STANLEY KANDLECAKE

Jeffery Tarry

Matador
9 Priory Business Park
Kibworth Beauchamp
Leicestershire LE8 0RX, UK
Tel: (+44) 116 279 2299
Fax: (+44) 116 279 2277
Email: books@troubador.co.uk
Web: www.troubador.co.uk/matador

ISBN 978 1783062 324

British Library Cataloguing in Publication Data.
A catalogue record for this book is available from the British Library.

Typeset in Aldine401 BT Roman by Troubador Publishing Ltd
Printed and bound in the UK by TJ International, Padstow, Cornwall

Matador is an imprint of Troubador Publishing Ltd

LOVE WILL TRIUMPH
OVER DEATH'S TEARS

CHAPTER ONE

The thin moon's crescent light flickered on the wet slate roofs of terraced houses and crept along the endless lines of parked cars jammed each side of the treeless street. Thick net curtains, impenetrable and inquisitive, stared at each other with unblinking superiority across the narrow, dark street built in a different century for iron hooves. The horse manure had been replaced by a graveyard of demolished car wing mirrors.

Behind the blistered door of number 97, Stanley Kandlecake's salivating chewed fingernail, ingrained with black engine oil, edged down the columns of 'Women seeking Men' with trembling anticipation.

They cried out to him from the newspaper with desperate tears that smudged the black ink. The teenage single mothers and the recently divorced. All hurt in the past by an uncaring, heartless bastard who had moved on to their ex-best friend or a local ladyboy. All needing someone to mend their broken hearts. "Oooh, complicated."

The exotic and the uninhibited, seeking an older male to satisfy…"Mmmh, interesting." Men who like the feel of leather. "Not quite sure about that one. Don't discount it though." The voluptuous and the sensual, seeking a real man.

A naughty man. A tactile man. "Tactile, what the hell is that? Something barmy queer."

Then he found her…Miss bloody gorgeous seeking bla… bla…bla…looks unimportant. "Hope she means that." He would give her a bell. Nothing to lose.

He pushed his inebriated body out of the sagging armchair and staggered over to a hexagonal pine mirror, hoping it's pitted surface would distort the unkind reflection. Staring back at him was a large crooked nose, matching ears and a wide mouth, too wide for the gaunt face. His dark oak eyes, framed in long lashes looked bizarre in that face, as if stolen from a beauty queen while she slept. Spread-eagled across the top of his head was a squashed 'daddy long legs' and next to him, a squashed close relative.

He turned his head for a side shot. The dangling legs tickled the top of his red ear and for some reason he arched his eyebrows. He looked a bit like that bloke who used to be on the telly a lot. Before he died, of course. He glanced in the mirror again and pulled a face. After he died?

"I've seen worse, much worse" and raised his chipped mug of dark rum at the grinning poster boy. The grin exploded into laughter and he collapsed onto a tangerine leatherette sofa. The curious material, prematurely aged by cracks and splits squeaked with every movement. He let the dark rum warm his brain and hoped the creatures on the wall could give him answers to the emptiness he felt inside.

He squinted at the gaily painted Chinese, Swiss cuckoo clock clinging to a nervous bent nail. The doors had jammed shut after the trusting cuckoo had been catapulted out on it's maiden leap. Now the unhappy bird hung upside down, suspended on a coiled spring, defiantly cuckooing on the hour but the doors refused to let her back in.

His eyes continued along the wall to an old friend, the last of three yellow beaked ducks. After an epic ten year voyage across the wall two had crash landed with exhaustion. The lonely survivor, it's velvet green head straining towards the door, beat his wings in a last desperate flight for freedom.

The empathy he felt for the luckless cuckoo and the uneatable duck was real because he was on the same flight path.

Half a century upon this earth and he had tasted only his own tears. A fear of the future replicating his past had crowbarred into his head. Every day spirited into a lost illusion. The armed robbers had squatters rights and could not be dislodged.

Ahead, another fifteen joyous years in the brickyard, a pat on the back, frog marched into senile obscurity and then dragged into a cul-de-sac for the inevitable and obscene disconnection of everything. The soul survives, he was certain of that.

"Oh sod it, come on you cheerful bugger, have another drink." He leaned over the back of the sofa, parted the yellowed lace curtains and peered through the gap. She would not be home for another hour, it was bingo night. So, time to change the future tonight, make that call to 'Miss Gorgeous.'

Fresh dark rum sloshed into the empty mug. He squinted at the advert. Eleven digits and then five box number digits. Total concentration was now required. He jabbed each number with mind boggling co-ordination, sipped his rum and waited.

Years dragged by. The ringing continued. "Come on, come on." What was this costing? "Bloody rip off." It continued to ring. Nothing. What an anticlimax. He positioned his finger over the 'Off' button.

"Hello." The voice in his reddened ear startled him.

"Oh, err, hello, I'm Stanley…"

"My name is Jenny and I'm looking for…" The pre-recorded voice talked over him.

Suddenly the front door gyrated open.

"Sodding hell." He jumped up like a startled frog.

A voice from the hall carried through. "Stanley, when are you going to fix this door? It's getting worse. We won't be able to open or close it at this rate."

"Err…" He hit the off button and scrambled around in panic. "You're early." He heard the door shudder and fell onto the sofa. "It's all this wet weather, it swells it."

Edith's face was flushed with the damp night air and winning bingo numbers. "We've had a wonderful evening." and plonked herself next to him. "What have you been up to all night?" Before he could answer she loosened her top. "Turn the gas fire down love, you can't breathe in here."

He glanced at the creature from the Pleistocene age crouched among the cracked tiles of the grey and cream fireplace. It hissed back at him, daring him to come closer. He cowered away from it's scorching heat and crunched the control to off. The warped radiants turned orange with a mad click, click, click. "The beast is put to bed."

"Tell me then" she continued.

He looked down at the tobacco he was rolling between his fingers. "Nothing much, usual rubbish on the telly." He licked the thin paper along it's length and finished rolling the cigarette. "Fancy a cuppa?"

"Ooh, this is a first, very thoughtful of you Stanley love."

He escaped into the tiny kitchen. Above him, polystyrene tiles gazed down in expectation of a single flame that would turn them into glamorous dripping fireballs. Bright yellow woodchip wallpaper, reinforced with six coats of thick emulsion clung to the walls with super glue ferocity. Only an industrial blowtorch could remove it's death grip. It's what the polystyrene tiles were praying for.

"Stanley" she called through to him, "would you say this old girl's still got it?"

The hot locomotive kettle puffed out steam into the claustrophobic space. It was an awkward moment. "Well, yes of course" and pulled a face. He poured the bubbling water into a house shaped teapot and wrapped it in a multi-coloured tea cosy.

"You know Mr Sinclair, the retired electrician, he's been giving me compliments all night. Paid for all my bingo cards It's just…when you reach a certain age…"

"85 is not old."

"I'm not that old you cheeky so and so."

"Tea made with love. Let it mash, I'm away in my dreams now. I'm on early shift."

"Thank you Stanley love, see you in the morning."

He bent over and kissed her on the forehead. "Goodnight mum."

On the other side of the plastered brick wall, inside No. 95, Cynthia Cramphorne brushed her long hair, unconcerned it was now thinner and whiter than last year. She was sitting in a brown wicker chair, staring out of the bedroom window at the red solar lights glowing in the dark garden and breathing in the night scent of fresh rain.

She moistened her palms and fingers. A ladies hands should be slender and delicate. These were made for 16 ounce boxing gloves. She loathed them. A sudden breeze lifted strands of her hair and she sighed. "Bedtime young lady." When she pushed her six foot gaunt figure out of the chair her wide shoulder blades jutted through her cotton nightdress like wooden coat hangers.

She made herself comfortable under the combined weight of four wool blankets and a thick candlewick bedspread. Her grey eyes followed the crescent moon until it edged beyond the dark glass. She snuggled up to a fluffy, putrid orange ape. "Night, night Stanley, sleep tight." Then kissed it's grinning mouth.

The loose wire inside her head had become detached years earlier, probably after burying her third husband. Most days the wire hung in solitary confinement, a harmless, twitching corpse but sometimes the raw end sparked against her skull, The crackling red flashes in the darkness could fuse the whole circuit. Finding it would be a problem. Best left alone.

The bed warmed up, the stars fragmented on the wet glass and Cynthia, the grinning orange ape and the loose wire, all dripping in medication, drifted away on a mothball scented pillow.

CHAPTER TWO

The ticking weapon of mass destruction, masquerading as an alarm clock exploded without warning inside Stanley's head. He diffused it with a wild swat and in the ringing silence swore he would get even one day. A recycled cremation was too good for that sadistic fat faced twat.

He swung his legs out of the bed. Stale dark rum sloshed against his brain, reactivating the buzzing bomb. The thought of another twelve hour shift sitting in his fork lift truck, loading thousands of bricks almost sobered him and his aching eyes tried to focus on the rain splattering down his window.

"Sod it." He crawled back under his crumpled warm duvet.

His mother's voice echoed up the stairs. "Stanley, breakfast nearly ready, *wakey wakey*." Then continued humming along to 'Sunrise Radio.'

"I'm awake." How could she be so cheerful at this ungodly hour? It wasn't normal.

Ten minutes later his bare feet stepped carefully on his crooked shadow being thrown down the stairs by a dusty, flickering light bulb. He slumped down at a red Formica laminate table, it's once bright, indestructible surface now dull and scratched but constructed to outlive everything on earth. The parlour panelled door, hidden behind tacked on hardboard and embellished with beheaded plastic coat hooks stared back at him in looking glass purple. The perfect colour for a hangover.

All five feet and seven stones of Edith's humming energy clattered through the exotic hanging plastic strips which separated the kitchen and dining room. Her size 2 'sensible' sneakers made no sound, not wishing to disturb the lime green and burnt orange carpet making violent love on the floor. The kaleidoscope of colour swirled from room to room around the vulnerable furniture in a giddy dance. Stanley's brain swayed with the rocking motion.

"Morning love, what have you done to your face?"

Bloody scraps of toilet paper were stuck to the cuts on his tender skin, freshly butchered by a new razor. "Hand's a bit unsteady this morning."

"Tea's mashed, don't let it stew." Steaming soft boiled eggs appeared, sitting snug and upright in their thin plastic cups.

Stanley and his mother, Edith, did not belong in the 21st century. Having survived *the* meteorite, the pair of domesticated, wingless pterodactyls, not quite ready for the abattoir shuffled and padded around their time locked 1960's Victorian terrace. Stanley in his oversize slippers with worn down heels, singing crazy cowboy songs and his mother in her size 2 snazzy sneakers and jazzy ankle socks. Both *tut-tutting* at the early morning horror movie, broadcasting live from Butsaswaland or some such unpronounceable, God-forsaken place.

Riots, earthquakes, financial meltdowns, atrocities in war zones. The global carnage was ladled over their cornflakes to the rhythms of Edith's humming *'tut, tut, tuts.'*

Their war was the snapping alligator letterbox, regurgitating overdue reminders. Money for this and money for that.

"Try and sort these out Friday, Stanley love." She dropped the week old, unopened demands on the table. "I think the rent is due this week."

He dipped his hot toasted 'soldiers' into the runny yoke and let it melt in his dehydrated mouth, trying to ignore the neighbour coughing up one of his lungs.

"Hark at him. You ought to think about cutting down a bit."

He nodded. 'Miss gorgeous' was whispering in his ear. He would try phoning her again tonight while Edith was at bell ringing practice. His mum would not approve or even understand. Anyway, no sense in upsetting her. His quest for a woman had not yet become obsessive but Stanley was a long way down the river.

He was late. He gulped down his tea, pushed the last piece of toast into his mouth and grabbed his 'pack up.' "What is it?"

"Haslet today love."

Haslet? Dried fly shit was more appealing. The silver foil parcel was destined for the best fed swans canal swans in England. Thursday was 'Tandori special' in the works café. "Thanks mam" and he kissed her on the forehead. "See you tonight."

"The weather's awful, drive careful love."

He freed the door from it's swollen grip and stumbled into icy blasts of rain. It felt like a rabid dog biting into his face. He winced as the scraps of toilet paper were ripped from his cuts and flung down the street. Inside his 1990 Ford Sierra, a spoilt only child, the gobbled breakfast burnt his chest and his dull, aching head hoped it wasn't going to be one of those days.

They lay in wait for him every morning. A cloned succession of monstrous road humps, easily mistaken for congealed fiery afterbirths from a mile below the earth's crust. This brotherhood of road dwellers were designed by a madman to last a thousand years. They were part of 'the problem.' An ongoing loathing close to hatred set off his palpitations. One of these days he would dynamite the lot.

The car rose and fell in scraping shrieks over each psychotic impregnation, in time but out of tune with Stanley's screaming curses. The murderous cluster of spine snapping concrete lumps left Stanley hoarse and the traumatised Sierra limped away suffering only whiplash.

He joined the happy melee of jostling motorists being carried to work on a blinding spray of rainwater. His lateness forced him to take a short cut through a 'dodgy area.'

The sky darkened and the rain clattered on his sun roof. He flicked his headlights on. They lit the faded arrows painted on another set of humps. Screaming was futile. Contagious as a medieval plague the brotherhood struck indiscriminately. Blocks of white flaking rendered houses crawled by. A stone clad house adorned with a wooden stagecoach wheel framed in black tudor beams startled him.

The 'Noah's Ark' deluge poured off vast solar panels dominating some of the roofs and flooded the overgrown front gardens, landscaped with bright red telephone boxes and engineless cars balanced on concrete blocks.

A bedraggled bunch of hunter/gatherers with a gaggle of their young shuffled across the road. The females only distinguishable by their breasts and more numerous tattoos. Stanley remained very quiet and still as if he were in the

Serengeti. If only he had a camera. What were they looking for? A woolly mammoth, perhaps. He wondered if David Attenborough knew about this place.

The limping Ford Sierra edged back into a stagnant queue of red brake lights. Stanley closed his eyes. So much for short cuts. He doubted if he would survive the day.

By the time he had parked outside Mr. Jamal's newsagents he was an hour late. He rushed through the deluge for tobacco and threw himself back into the car. If he had been swimming with the swans in the canal he could not be any wetter. He folded the small pink ticket for last night's winning lottery and lined up the numbers with his lucky birthday numbers. Ten years loyalty had paid out two £10 wins.

Hunched over the steering wheel he compared each winning number and his birthday numbers. He stared in disbelief. Surely not. It can't be. He placed his finger on each number again. Across and down. Up, across and down, with shorter, heavier breaths his eyes followed his slow, robotic finger, digesting each number. There was no doubt, absolutely no doubt. He flopped back into his seat, holding both tickets at arm's length, screwed up his face and cried out with the insane laughter of a man looking at his own gravestone. "You would think just one. Not one, not one bloody number and let the tickets flutter from his hands.

Stanley and his forklift truck sat half a mile apart in the pouring rain, both in a foul mood, both hating each other's guts.

Their marriage was on the rocks. Stanley had taken too many blows to the head. Punch drunk from too many lorry diesel fumes, too many reversing bleep, bleep, bleeps, too many bricks, much too many bricks. He wanted out of this partnership.

They were a double act. The ventriloquist and the dummy. Which one was *HE* ? Today he felt like the grinning head on a stick. Perhaps he had always played that part.

He began rolling a cigarette. The truck waited with growing impatience. "OK, I'm coming. Just having a smoke, if that's all right with you." But it was not alright, he was over an hour late and he felt tugging on his neck. "You think I'm a loser, don't you? Do you think that bothers me? It doesn't. Nothing you think or say bothers me. Sorry…Speak up…Oh, really…" The rain thundered down on the roof of the car and drowned out all conversation.

CHAPTER THREE

Stanley's eyes jerked open. Where was he, what happened? Still in the car, he had just dozed off and he snatched at his watch. He had dozed for an hour. "You idiot prat."

He turned the ignition key. The starter motor whirred and jolted the engine but the pistons refused to fire. "Please, not today. Start… Please."

Nine times he pleaded with each turn of the key until the battery made a slow motion groan. He slumped back, closed his eyes and puffed out his cheeks. Why had he bothered getting out of bed this morning? Not owning a mobile phone and not being a member of any roadside rescue did not help. He would have to walk. Have a smoke first to calm down. He reached into his pocket and some loose coins and a small pink butterfly scattered over the floor. It was just an old lottery ticket.

His head was thick with snatched sleep and just about everything else. He struggled with the window winder. Stale smoke collided with the cool wet air rushing in and he sucked it all up as he unfolded the crumpled lottery ticket. It was his mother's. She had kept the same numbers for the last ten years. The date was for last Saturday but he could still compare the numbers to Wednesday's draw.

He held the two sets of numbers together. Number 1 matched, 3 matched and 11 matched. The remaining three numbers on her ticket were creased, almost erased. "Sod it." Somewhere in the glove compartment was a magnifying glass. His hand groped among the furry dice and furry apple cores. "Gotcha."

He scanned the glass over the three remaining winning numbers. 18 was the first one. He panned down to Edith's Saturday ticket. The number was just legible. 18. It matched. "Yes." The glass moved back up. 25, then hovered over her fifth number. Squinting hard through the magnification at the creased, faded digits, the number blurred. He looked away, rubbed his right eye and blinked until it focused. Closing his left eye, he lowered the glass and his head over the ticket, straining his right eye to lift the two numbers off the pink paper. The chewed digits knitted together for a split second mating ritual. 25. "They match. Dear God."

What was the last number on the winning line? 49. He held the magnifying glass over his mother's last number. It was either 38 or 48 or 39 or…49. The glass was moved up and down over the creased faded number. His right eye ached and everything became a watery blur. "Damn." His head throbbed, it seemed impossible.

She had definitely matched five numbers. How much had she won? The small 'void not for sale' ticket printed Match 5/6. Winners Count 250. Pays £2,328.00. "Fantastic." What about the big one?

Match 6/6 Winners Count 1 Pays £7,856,322.00. "Dear God."

A horrible thought passed through him. He hoped and prayed he was wrong. He suddenly remembered his mother telling him she had forgotten to buy a ticket before going to bingo last night.

"Oh God, no please." Did she tell him that? He was hung over this morning. Now he wasn't sure. If that last number came up it was 'throw yourself under a bus time.' With fresh eyes he held the glass over that last number. It began to look like 49 and he remembered now. She did tell him and that number was 49. He covered his face with his hands and almost brought up his breakfast. Head down, he hung on to the dashboard, shaking with panicking horror.

Someone was speaking through the open window. " Stanley, are you all right?" It was Mr Jamal, the newsagent, standing under an umbrella. Stanley nodded. "You left this on the counter yesterday, I forgot to give it to you earlier." He handed a black purse through the opening. "Sure you're alright?"

"Fine." Stanley croaked and Mr Jamal, distracted by the downpour of rain, hurried back to his shop.

Paralysed with shock in the desolation of his car, he could taste the rising vomit in his throat. He wanted to cry but could not. He wanted his life to end now, enough was enough, this was the last cruel act. He felt the blade of his pocket penknife. It was always kept sharp, more than adequate for what it had to do. Who would miss him? He twiddled with the clasp of his mother's black purse and then he began to sob.

The effort left him gasping, his nose streamed, his body trembled and he gripped the steering wheel with numb hands, head down, eyes closed.

His poor mother. He would not tell her, the shock might kill her. It had damn near killed him. He looked down at her purse in his lifeless fingers and could not even remember taking it out but he must have. He flicked it open and pulled out a small 'lotto fast pay card' in a plastic cover, the one he always used to buy his lottery ticket. A clip was attached to it and he turned it over. On the underside was a folded lottery ticket. He must have bought two by mistake or Saturday's in advance. No, it was for Wednesday, last night's draw. Puzzled, he turned it over again. The numbers were not his, it was not his 'lotto fast pay card.' Puzzled and now confused he turned it over again and unfolded the lottery ticket. The numbers were familiar. They looked like his mother's numbers but how could they be?

The last number screamed out at him. 49. Was it his mother's ticket? He could not take much more of this. "Calm, take deep breaths." With renewed shaking he compared the numbers again. 1....3....11....18....25....and...49.

In his trembling hand was the only winning jackpot lottery ticket for last night's draw. "Dear God."

It was his mother's ticket. He must have handed over her 'Lotto Pay Card' with his own, yesterday, by mistake. He could not remember, he did not care. He felt totally disorientated. Was this real? Had he fallen asleep again? Was he awake or just dreaming?

He struck a match and held his palm over the flame. "Aaahh." The pain was real, this was real. He could not get enough oxygen into his lungs. His elephant ears became blood red pressure cookers, his crooked nose throbbed, somebody repeatedly jabbed a pin in his heart. This time he was going to die.

After a few minutes he was only hyper-ventilating. He checked the numbers and the date again. They all matched. There was no mistake. £7,856,322.00.

"Dear God, 7.8 million."

What was left of him dissolved in a bubbling puddle between the accelerator and the brake pedal.

The whirling dervish that was once Stanley Kandlecake catapulted out of the car door into the biblical deluge. With arms outstretched he twirled across the pavement like a 'song and dance' movie star from an old Hollywood musical and napalmed two teenage schoolgirls hurrying by under a large umbrella. Both screamed in unison, the umbrella flipped into the air and all three crashed to the ground in a sprawling tangled mess. One of the girl's lashed out with a wild kick. She connected with the umbrella and it cart wheeled down the road.

"You moron." It was an out of breath howl "What were you doing?"

"I'm sorry, I'm sorry, it was an accident."

"It's not funny, why are you laughing?"

"I'm not, let me help you up."

"Don't touch me, I'll call the police."

"Yes, call the police Bethy" her friend scrambled to her feet.

"No, don't do that Bethy, I really am sorry. It's been a strange day. Please, let me help you."

"Piss off."

"Fair enough." He stepped back from the two drowned she-wolves.

"He's still laughing Bethy."

"Moronic prat." Turning arm in arm they scuttled away after their umbrella.

"Sorry." He waved as they fled into the monsoon and knelt down on the flooded pavement. Laughing hysterically, with the rain pouring off his upturned face and his drenched T-shirt clinging to his bruised rib cage he raised both grazed arms to the grey heavens.

"Thank you, dear Lord, thank you."

Watching from the shop doorway, Mr. Jamal shook his head and called to his wife.

Stanley staggered back to his car, both arms still raised, fingers pointing at the stormy heavens.

Mr. Jamal turned to his wife and a smiling customer, all crowded in the doorway. "He's harmless."

His wife raised her eyebrows. "You think so?"

He shrugged. "Yes, I think so." His wife shook her head.

Stanley ducked inside his car and sat motionless, unable to move, speak or even think. Steam rose from his saturated clothing, fogging up the windows.

"You won't believe it mum. I don't believe it." He started laughing, a coughing, spluttering, choking spasm. His nose and eyes streamed, blurring the cigarette he had started to roll with damp, trembling fingers. "You just won't believe it mum."

He wiped away the 'fog' from his windscreen and watched the rain turn to freezing sleet. Minutes later a white storm of large hailstones bounced off his roof and bonnet. He started singing "England in the Springtime, la, la la." The lighted end of his fat, bent 'roll up' glowed as he sucked it's sweet contents deep into his sub-conscious. He tilted back his head, closed his watery eyes and listened to the deafening roar.

After a while he slipped the lottery ticket and lotto card into the lucky black purse.

He turned the ignition key and the battery growled in slow motion. The engine shuddered with life and a whoop filled the car. Half a gallon of four star unleaded was revved through the exhaust in high celebration. The heater wafted warm air over his wet, cold body and he joined the returning remnants of the school run.

The Sierra was like a cat, not imitating his graceful

movements but marking his territory with spraying oil. This slick was carried away down a storm drain.

This new world for the multi-millionaire was a confusion of clattering rain, insane whoopee's, delirious laughter and swirling cigarette smoke. What if he collected the whole 7.8 million now, in £20 notes. Would it fit in the car? No, he would have to return, three or four times. "Yeehaa."

He sang along with the frantic swish of the window wipers. "Seven point eight, la, la, la," Swish, swish, swish. "Seven point eight."

He sucked in more tobacco. Concentrate. Watch the speed limit. No short cuts. The smoke stung his eyes. No begging letters please. No hard luck stories. No new friends or worse, new relatives. They would make just one big bonfire. What about women? He wasn't that fussy, anything really between 17 and 70 but he would have his pick. Wouldn't he? He glanced in the rear view mirror. Perhaps not. A bit of surgery would sort that problem out. Don't be a prat. His happy smile became a £7.8 million lunatic's grin. Nothing could spoil this moment, Nothing.

CHAPTER FOUR

Nurse Sue Joggle stepped out of the stifling heat of the A&E hospital and welcomed the rain splattering against her face. Another nightshift finally over. These ungodly hours and being the wrong side of forty only gave her headaches and heartburn.

Her husband, Dominic, was another worry. Something was not quite right, for a couple of months or more now. How long since they had made love? About the same. He was possibly still depressed after his business was declared bankrupt. She was not imagining it, he was not the same man she had married less then a year ago. She would try and talk to him again this morning. Hopefully he would be in a better mood than last night. She hated arguments. Her first marriage was row after row and could not face that again but she would have to say something.

Driving home through the deluge, she was distracted by an old white car, just visible, in front of her, driving without lights. "In these conditions. Idiot." It disappeared after overtaking a slow flashing orange light. The milk float turned off and she followed the old car onto a big roundabout.

If only Dominic would……

The foreign twelve wheeled monster was lost. It's

headlights could see other headlights but hidden in a wall of water was a speeding blind pensioner.

Stanley was deafened by a ship's warning claxon horn and never heard the grinding metal death plunge of his Sierra. He was trapped inside, upside down, his legs twisted at strange angles, water coming in. He would drown. His body trembled with the vibration of a monster diesel engine. The sweet smile of petrol terrorised his shattered senses.

Sue's right foot stamped down on the brake pedal and she gripped the steering wheel in horror. The car screeched in a frenzied dance around the embracing, twisted metal. It stopped only yards away. Still in shock, she grabbed her phone and punched in 999.

"Hello, emergency, which service do you require?"

Sue shouted over the thunderous rain to the calm voice and was assured they were on their way. She jumped out of the car and slipped on the wet, greasy road. Stunned by the fall, lying in a moving rainbow of oil and water amongst the debris, a small black purse bobbled against her hand. She instinctively grabbed it and pushed it into her coat pocket.

An approaching siren cut into ears. Flickering blue lights rebounded off everything.

"Are you hurt?" It was a policewoman

"No, I'm alright." Supported by the policewoman she limped back to her car.

When Sue finally opened the door of her semi-detached house she was still shaking and could hardly remember the journey home. She called up the stairs when she heard the muffled bedroom TV. "Dominic, are you awake?"

He stretched out his long legs under the quilt and turned up the volume. No, he mouthed, yawned and his thoughts returned to the bad luck that had followed him around like a recurring dose of haemorrhoids, breaking out at the most vulnerable moments. The failed businesses, his debts. Other people had let him down. He could not be held responsible for their incompetence, their weaknesses.

His wife opened the bedroom door. "I've been trying to ring you."

"I didn't hear it" he lied.

"I'm not surprised, can you turn it down please."

"You have fathered five children by five different women." the angry host accused the teenager.

"What a dildo." Dominic laughed.

"Dominic, please listen. You won't believe what happened to me this morning." The clamouring mothers at the bottom of the bed drowned her out.

"What? I was listening to that." The TV was silenced.

"Thank you. There was a terrible accident on the big roundabout. Happened right in front of me. The road is still blocked. I had to give statements to the police, that's why I'm late."

"Anybody hurt?" He was watching the soundless TV.

"A man. They had to cut him free. He looked badly injured."

"Well, if he makes it, you can nurse him through the night."

"Yes, I suppose I can Dominic."

"There you go then, cherub."

"Don't call me cherub, you know I don't like it."

"Ooohh, a bit touchy, aren't we."

"Yes we are. So would you be."

"Look, have a shower, take some happy pills and you'll feel better."

"You can be a real dickhead, do you know that?"

22

"All I'm saying is, get some sleep, things will seem better."

"No Dominic, they won't, that's what I want to talk to you about. Look at me."

He lifted his eyes away from the TV. She looked wider and plainer than yesterday. Nightshifts did not suit her. "Not now, I have to be at the Job Centre in an hour."

"Tonight then, before my shift."

"I'll be out all day, so I won't disturb you."

"How thoughtful. I'll see you tomorrow then."

"You will cherub."

She ignored him, shook her head and flounced out the room. He stared at the photo of the beauty on their wedding day. She had been on a diet ever since that photo was taken. It was her fault he didn't fancy her any more. He looked away and smiled with excited anticipation at the coming night.

He was a man's man. The full length mirror told him so. He posed naked in front of it, legs apart, hands on hips and nodded with approval. A love stud. He turned around and glanced over his shoulder. Everything muscular, everything tight without flexing. He pushed a hand through his long black hair. He felt aroused. You can't fake that and nodded again.

When Sue climbed into the bed he was gone. She watched the silent TV and waited for the tablets to hit.

Dominic stood astride his new, very expensive cycle and pressed the phone close to his ear, shouting above the din of evening traffic. "Hi babe, it's me."

"Hi, are you still coming over?"

"Yeah, I've just left the gym, be there in about an hour. I'll pick up a pizza on the way and a bottle of something."

" Everything all right?"

"Yeah, yeah, still love me?"

"Of course I do."

"Love you babe."

"I know, see you later."

"See you later alligator."

Dominic launched his missile into the evening rush hour giving the one finger salute to a tooting car. His long dark hair streamed around his silver framed black sunglasses. He was a scarlet red lycra daredevil on a silver flying machine, skimming between the brawling metal and noise and tunnels of low, blinding sunlight in the shadows of the city

Style. He had it. Most ignoramus's were not even aware of it's existence. Style. No-one could take that away from him.

He jumped a red light, startling a smart suited idiot. "Peasant" he yelled. Before the open mouthed woman could reply, the red and silver torpedo was gone.

Sue Joggle forced her body out of the warm bed, her head reeling with undigested sleeping pills, bad dreams and interrupted sleep. Her phone rang. "Hello."

"You sound rough."

"Is that you Dominic?"

"It could be. Look, sorry about this morning, we'll talk tomorrow. Alright?"

She sighed, "Yes, alright. Where are you?"

"Just on my way to the gym."

"It is important that we talk about this."

"Got to go. Try not to kill anyone tonight,"

Before she could say 'Dickhead' the phone clicked off.

CHAPTER FIVE

Was he dead? Alone and in absolute terror, Stanley was tumbling through eternity. Lost in a dark red growling emptiness. Orbiting beyond his outstretched fingers were his amputated legs, separated white mutations. Broken, floppy, obscene.

He grabbed one. It wriggled free from his weak grip with a child's giggle and spun away with ferocious flips.

The effort exhausted him. Gasping for air, he was falling faster and faster. It became too painful to breathe. A rich blackness, silent and peaceful, wrapped around him. The blanket was soothing and comforting. He fell asleep.

Then he heard them. Voices, faraway. What did they want? He did not care, he was too tired and he felt no connection to them. Go away, let me sleep.

A tremendous jolt blasted through his body. His whole skeleton was visible, lit from within by a searing white hot flash.

Air forced open his flat, dusty lungs. They billowed in hurried gulps and wedged, shrieking against his ribcage. Blood, thick and black, rampaged through abandoned veins. The flooded tubes stretched and bulged in agony. The world's oceans roared in his ears. His left leg had been welded on the wrong side of his body.

That's when he heard something gnawing on his shin bone.

"For God's sake, stop."

The pain drained away. He could hear it dripping into a bucket. He lost count at 78. 78? What was that? Sleepy peace filtered through him. Not the profound perfection of earlier. This was spoiled by nonsensical speech and sharp stabbing needles. His cactus tongue dreamt of cold frothy beer.

"Rest now Stanley love." The voice was closer now.

'Yes I think I will.' He felt happy again, having found his missing legs.

"God bless."

The two nurses were whispering over the wreckage encased in bandages and plaster. A steady bleep told them he was alive.

"What's his name?" Sue was back on her shift.

"Stanley Kandlecake."

"Kandlecake?"

"Yes" her friend smiled, "He's stable now, we almost lost him earlier."

So this was the man from the accident this morning. Sue held her breath. She was lying in the half flooded road, swimming with rainbows of petrol, surrounded by deafening sirens, flashing blue rain, mangled debris and the air knocked out of her body.

She exhaled and breathed in the smells of the warm hospital. Unclenching her hand, she stared down at a small black purse in her palm. She shivered and it disappeared. Where was it?

Minutes later she rummaged through her coat pockets

hanging in the locker. Nothing. She tried to remember. It was this coat and she had put the purse in one of the pockets. She pushed her hand in again and her fingers poked through a hole in the lining Squeezing all her fingers inside the lining she gripped something. Is this it? She tugged it through the hole. It was the black purse. Did it belong to Stanley 'whatisname'?

She flicked open the catch. It was empty. Just a folded lottery ticket, a 'Lotto Fast Pay Card' and the winning lottery numbers on another ticket from last night's draw. It was impossible to resist, she unfolded the lottery ticket and checked the numbers.

The dates matched. Her eyes jumped from side to side like balls in a pinball machine. Her hysterical stomach strangled her heart and leapt into the back of her throat. The numbers matched.

"Oh my God."

All the oxygen was sucked out of the room. The pink tickets wobbled in her hands.

Someone removed her kneecaps and she crashed against the wall. Falling over was becoming a bad habit. On shocked legs she reached the window, fumbled it open and gulped in the cold Spring night with grateful breaths.

A siren disturbed the low hum of traffic and she closed the window with numb fingers. She was still alone in the cloakroom and checked the numbers and dates again.

She was looking at a jackpot winning ticket. Absolutely no doubt. This was really happening. Did it tell her the winning amount? No. The evening local paper lay folded on a chair. Would it be in there? She flicked through the pages, eyes running up and down the columns. Surely they print it. Her stomach performed a handstand then somersaulted across the room.

'One lucky winner scoops Wednesday's Jackpot Draw.'
£7,856,322.00.

"Oh my God." The paper fell to the floor and she covered her face with both hands.

"There you are Sue. Are you all right?"

Her body jumped. "Err…Yes… Fine…It's just a headache."

"You are wanted in Ward 6. Is that your purse on the floor?"

Sue gaped at the small black object. "Yes."

"It's sheer madness tonight. Have fun."

"Thanks Julie." She was alone again. She picked up the purse, carefully placed the tickets inside and secured it in her uniform pocket. She wandered down to Ward 6 with comatose steps. Life goes on and so does death.

"Hello."

"Hi Lucy, it's Sue." There was a long pause. "Hello."

"Yes, hello. Sorry Sue, it's a bad line."

"Don't like bothering you at this late hour but I'm trying to contact Dominic. You don't know the number or name of his gym do you?" His mobile's switched off and there is no answer on the landline."

"No idea. Sorry. I only know it's an expensive place. He never phones here. Is it urgent?"

"Well, quite urgent but don't be concerned, It's nothing to worry about. I'll tell you everything tomorrow. Take care."

"And you."

"Tell me again what she said." Dominic was biting his bottom lip.

"She wanted the name and number of your gym because your phone is switched off and no reply at home. Said it was urgent but nothing to worry about and would tell me everything tomorrow. That's it."

"It's alright, I think I know what it's all about, she's been moaning like shit all week. I'll sort it out in the morning." He thought for a moment and frowned. "How did she sound?"

"For God's sake Dominic, she sounded fine."

"She didn't sound…*Offish*?"

"No, if anything she sounded excited. I know her well enough by now."

"You should do. She is your sister."

"How could she know anything, we've been too careful. Now stop worrying, I'm gagging for some cock."

"How quaint." He was watching Lucy undress from a leather armchair.

Her black dress fell to the floor and she sauntered towards him. Half her body, lit by a shaded glass lamp, was milkshake pink. The other half, shadowy curves. She inched closer. Blond scraped back hair, mauve lips, dark erect nipples, white panties. He reached out and she drew back, breasts swaying in cupped hands.

"You teasing bitch."

She smiled and kneeled down between his legs. "Sorry baby. Tell Lucy where it hurts." She slid both hands up his thighs, inside his silk boxer shorts. "Just there?"

"Yes."

"Lets have a closer look." She pulled down his shorts and he kicked them free. "Do you want me to kiss it better."

"Yes." He held her blond hair as it bobbed up and down. "Slow and hard babe." He tilted back his head and groaned "Perfect."

She looked up and smiled again.

"Don't stop, please." She bit the inside of his thigh.

"You bitch. So you want it rough." He jumped up and positioned himself behind her. She squealed and leaned forward over the chair, head down, bracing her legs. She gasped at the first thrust of his arched back and low moan.

Her nails dug into the soft leather chair. "Fuck me Tarzan boy...... Fuck *meee.*"

The frenzied nightshift had exhausted itself. Most of the hospital was locked in an unfamiliar quiet murmur. The early morning sun felt brittle on Sue's face. She was looking at the half Egyptian Mummy brought back from the dead.

Was it his ticket? Deep down, she knew it was. What was she waiting for? His second demise? She suddenly felt disgust and shame. Tears ran down her face. It wasn't her ticket. She had stolen it. This poor man had suffered terrible injuries. A toxic guilt forced fresh tears into her eyes.

"Don't worry Sue, he's improving by the hour." The doctor was towing three students around. Embarrassed, she quickly wiped her face. He studied his notes. "The only concern I have is retrograde or anterograde amnesia."

She stared open mouthed at him. "You mean total memory loss?"

"Total or partial. With these injuries there is always a strong possibility." Before she could reply they had shuffled away to the next patient, talking to each other in low tones and scribbling on clip boards.

She brushed his swollen face with her fingertips. "Dear God, forgive me."

Sue blundered through her front door, exhausted with the same thoughts rotating like corkscrews inside her brain.

"So, what was the big problem last night?" Dominic's voice came from the kitchen.

She tried to clear her head. A puzzled expression spread across her face. Her voice was weary. "How did you know?"

"What?"

"That I was trying to reach you."

"The answer phone."

She looked even more puzzled. "But it's not working and your phone was switched off all night." She walked into the kitchen. "Well, who told you?"

"Must have been the gym receptionist."

"I couldn't find the number. The only person I told was Lucy." He fiddled with a carton of milk. "Did you hear me Dominic?"

"Yes. Sorry, I'm getting all mixed up. Lucy told me."

"But how could you if your phone's switched off. Anyway, she told me you never phone there and it must have been late."

He turned on the sink taps and squirted soap onto his hands. "Yes it was late. The battery's dead on my mine, so I used Tom Higgis's phone. You know Tom."

She looked at him, more perplexed than ever. "So why did you phone Lucy late at night?"

He shook his wet hands, glancing around for a towel. "Why?" He found the towel, coughed and covered his face with it.

"Yes, why?"

The towel was lowered. "There's free membership at the gym, only for a week. Thought she may be interested."

"Was she?"

"Said she was, then mentioned you wanted to speak to me. Tom had to leave, he was already late, so I could not call you"

"So why didn't you call me from home?

"Because I was tired and went straight to bed. I didn't think it was that important."

"I called half a dozen times, you must have heard it?"

He spread his arms out. "No. What's with all these stupid questions. Just tell me what the problem is."

She took a deep breath. "The problem, Dominic, is you. Something's been wrong for a while now and I want to know what it is."

"Nothing's wrong. You're the one with the problem. You're getting paranoid. It's working in that nuthouse that's doing it."

" Well one of us has to work."

"AH, AH. Now we're getting down to what's eating at your *craw.*"

"Don't try to twist things around."

"You're the one that's twisted. You need to have this looked at." He tapped her on the forehead with his finger, his dilated pupils only inches away from her face. "You know what you are?"

She stepped back. "What am I Dominic?"

He pushed his face into her face again. "A paranoid bitch, that's what."

She flinched at the poisonous spit and jumped at the recoil of the slamming door. Shaking with shock and anger, she shouted through the door. "If I'm a paranoid bitch, you're a …" She could not think of anything. The front door vibrated on it's hinges and she opened the window. "Can you hear me Dominic, you………Twat's arsehole."

He sprinted away on his cycle, ducking from the *Whizzbang* hurled at his head.

Sue held the pink lottery tickets and checked the dates and numbers for the sixth time, then checked the numbers in the folded newspaper. £7,856,322.00. She sipped the strong black coffee. If it was Stanley's ticket and if he did suffer total memory loss. What then? Who would know? Perhaps he had already told someone. It's not something you would want to keep a secret. But she had.

She could see the numbers being divided up between people she did not know and poor old Stanley might not know. She looked down at the numbers again.

£7,856,322.00. She would wait for a while and tell no-one and see what happens.

Lucy felt wrecked and so was her flat. This hangover was not her worst but it was a 'humdinger.' The evidence of Dominic's first all night 'stopover' was scattered all around her. Empty bottles, discarded clothing, bedding, pillows and the stink of burnt out candles. It had been a wild night.

The 'clean-up' could wait. She lit a cigarette and lowered herself into the rising steam of the overflowing bathwater. Her love of being submerged in scalding water left a poisonous sweat on her face. It trickled onto her lips and she licked it off with a yellowing tongue.

She drained the large mug of Bacardi/ coffee and drew hard on a fresh cigarette.

Now she felt alive again.

It was insanity carrying the ticket on her person. She would not walk around with eight million pounds in her handbag would she? It had to be hidden. Sue walked through the house. Where is the last place a burglar would look? It should be easy to conceal such a small item. Cupboards, drawers, inside books, inside vases? No. Taped inside one of the high picture rails? No. Where, where?

Then she remembered. The loose floorboard under the bedroom radiator, the leaking joint. She pulled back the carpet and levered out the short board with a cutlery knife. She sealed the purse and the 7.8 million pound ticket inside a small plastic container and pushed it an arm's length under the floor. Hidden behind a lump of old insulation it was perfectly camouflaged.

Itching and coughing from the yellow irritant she snapped the board back in place and trod the carpet back under the radiator. She felt like an ancient druid burying a gold relic. Something the invading Romans would never find.

Her phone rang. "Hi Sue, it's Lucy. Did you contact Dominic?"

"Yes, it's all sorted out now, thanks. Except he's gone off in a huff."

"He's in trouble then?"

"I don't know Lucy, recently he seems so cold and distant. He hasn't been near me for two months."

"Oh," Lucy tried not to smile. " He could be worried about something.."

"Yes, I thought about that." She paused for a moment. "You don't think he's carrying on behind my back do you?"

Now Lucy hesitated. "No, what makes you think that?"

"Women must find him attractive and he is such a flirt. Do you find him attractive Lucy?"

The line was silent for a couple of seconds. "Well, yes I suppose so. I think a lot of women do. He's not exactly ugly is he?"

"No, he's not. Anyway, it's not your problem."

"Don't be silly, if you want to talk, call me anytime."

"Thanks Lucy. Oh, I almost forgot. I'm visiting mother tonight. Do you want to come with me?"

"Err, I can't see the point and that place gives me the *eeby jeebies*. Sorry Sue, but I think it's a waste of time, I really do."

"It's all right, I understand. Let's meet for a coffee in town next week."

"That will be lovely, give me a ring. Bye then Sue."

"Bye Lucy." She smoothed the carpet under the radiator with her foot. No-one in the world knew it was there. Only her.

Lucy lit another cigarette. It was her birthday soon, the big 30. She would stay 29 forever. The nicotine was soothing. The affair with Dominic was never intended, it just happened. It did not feel wrong, only natural. He said he loved her, he made her feel happy and he shagged her silly. Right now she couldn't live without him.

Sue always felt a sickly anticipation before going in and a sickly relief coming out of the care home. Built in the 1970's, the large building had been renovated inside but the exterior cream rendering was cracked and flaking. A few fresh hanging baskets had been strung up each side of the door. It reminded her of bright baubles on a dead Christmas tree.

"Ah, you're here to see Eunice."

"How is she?"

The smart receptionist with a pleasant voice consulted her file. "Eunice is about the same since your last visit a week ago,. She is a very spirited lady and is eating well, with a little help and responds well to everything we ask. I think she's in the T.V. lounge. We can have a longer chat when you leave."

"Yes. Thanks." Sue stood in the lounge doorway and watched her mother shuffle towards her, head down, supported by a nurse. There was a new awkwardness in her movements, a new slowness, a new strain in her face.

"Hi mum." Sue whispered.

The lady named Eunice slowly raised her face and for

several seconds recognition sparked in her brown eyes, then it was ripped away.

With watery vision Sue watched her flop into a chair and close her eyes. A grey haired stranger, buried in a nightgown, among grey haired strangers watching the new all in one hair miracle on the big screen.

She almost laughed through choking tears and walked over to where she was dozing. The harmless, creased, baby child made tiny dreaming sounds and smelt of lavender. Sue bent over and kissed the pink skin under the thin grey strands.

"Goodnight mum, stay safe." The room was uncomfortably hot. She needed fresh air and rushed to the exit with her hand over her mouth. The bolted fish and chips, lodged at the back of her throat were spewed out over the floodlit lawn.

The caretaker, filling the rubbish bins, looked over and swore. "Bleedin ell, I only mowed that this morning."

"Sorry." she blurted out and escaped to her car. Recovering inside, a sudden connection between her mother and Stanley hit her. They both had memory loss. Stanley through a horrific car accident and her mother eaten away by Alzheimer's disease. Would she steal a fortune from her mum? Of course not.

Guilt battered her over the head again.

She watched the blinds being drawn over the brightly lit windows of the care home. The meaty bones from the sale of her mother's bungalow had been almost licked clean by the care fees. What would happen to mum when the account had been emptied? Sue had no savings, nothing valuable to sell.

The Alzheimer's would continue to devour mum's brain and body. There was no cure. She would need specialist's care, the very best treatment. She deserved no less but it would all be very expensive. It would need money. A lot more money.

The sadness and confusion left a sharp pain thumping over her eyes as she drove home through the black, wet night and she did not notice the heavy showers of rain trying to dissolve the yellow puddle of liquidised fish and chips, staining the much loved floodlit lawn.

CHAPTER SIX

Cynthia Cramphorne's articulate voice leapt over the low privet hedge. "Edith, would it be convenient for me to accompany you on your next hospital visit to see dear Stanley."

"Yes, of course Cynthia. I could do with some support."

"Dare I ask, how is he now?"

"Well, the swelling on his face has gone down and he can talk, just. He still can't remember anything that happened on the day of the crash but apart from that he's seems to be getting better, in himself."

"Oh, that is good news. How long has it been since that terrible day?"

"Nearly a week now."

"I do clearly recall the awful, absolutely awful, weather we suffered on that day. It reminded so very much of the day I buried poor Harry. Bless him. A different breed of men. Different times of course. Stanley has many of the same traits, being the tail end of that generation. All to be forgotten soon, as if we never existed, never breathed or loved, just gold letters on black marble that pigeons shit on. You are very fortunate indeed to have a son of Stanley's calibre. When would be an appropriate hour for hospital visiting?"

"Err, half past six alright?"

"I better go and prepare then. I do hope the poor boy is feeling better. I am a believer in the healing power that words of encouragement can bring. Do not concern yourself with transport Edith, I will hire a black hackney. Six thirty punctual, I shall tell him and to return here when we are ready. Now, where did I put those shoes?"

"Bye Cynthia."

Through the slatted blind, shards of sunlight cut into Stanley's eyelids. He heard a click and the bright pain was gone. He tried to force open his eyelids but his long lashes were glued together with white gunge. Something wet and warm wiped them clean and they fluttered open. The blurred outline of his mum's face was whispering to him. "Hello Stanley love. How are you feeling tonight?"

Only the thought of his head falling off prevented him from laughing. Every part of his body felt bruised or broken including the backs of his eyeballs. His swollen lips opened and slurred "Wha appended?"

"You have been in a car accident, Stanley love. The doctor's say you'll be just fine. You just need rest."

"Ow do I luk?" His features had taken on the appearance of a church roof gargoyle. That hideous vomiter of rainwater.

"A few cuts and bruises, nothing to worry about."

"I found my legs."

Her whispers were close to his whispers and a tear dropped onto the gargoyle's face. "Yes, I know love, you told me yesterday. You will feel much better tomorrow. That's what the doctors say, after a good night's sleep." He moved the fingers of the hand she was clasping with both her hands and gave a painful wink.

Cynthia held his other hand with a hand of similar

proportions. If he had known, he would have been afraid and when he heard her speak he was afraid but now he was too tired to be afraid and that was the scariest thing of all.

The dusky back room in the terraced house was silent except for Cynthia's loud blue and white flowered dress. The only other sounds were the polite crunching of a digestive biscuit and Edith's spoon clinking against a cup.

"You do brighten a room up Cynthia."

"Thank you dear." They were sitting each side of the red formica table. The scarred rescue dog was laid out for afternoon tea. Woolworth's finest white porcelain and the house shaped teapot were on display. Edith encased the pot in a multi coloured, crocheted tea cosy. It matched the one on her head.

She stirred the extra spoon of sugar into the hot lava of dark tea. "I could do with some more energy inside me. It's funny how quiet the house seems without Stanley clumping about."

"I think you are coping wonderfully dear." Cynthia spoke between genteel nibbles on her digestive. "Given these dreadful circumstances."

"I've been glad of your company this past week. it's been such a comfort. Kept me soldiering on."

"My dear Edith, when Harry passed away, your support was invaluable. I know it was some years ago now but I'll never forget your kindness."

Edith adjusted her red zig-zag ankle socks. "Oh, bless. I just can't get used to sleeping alone in the house. I'm so glad you're only next door."

"Loneliness. Yes, one could write a book. You have my sympathies dear. With Harry, what's the expression? 'Losing your grip on reality.' One adapts, of course and informed that living alone has it's advantages but I miss a man's …Touch. Yes, I think that's the right word. After all, without sounding vulgar, one can still function in that department, if you know what I mean."

"Well, yes I think so."

"The trials and tribulations we must endure, it's all so wearisome." She looked down at her plain gold ring. "I am surprised Stanley never married."

"He's come close a few times."

"Did you scare them off Edith?"

"No, I want him to be happy."

"I was only joking with you dear. What was the name of the last one?

"Denise."

"Denise, what a strange girl she was. The mad harpie I called her."

"She wasn't that bad. You mean hippie don't you?"

"No dear, I mean harpie, a mad troll if you like. Much too young for him anyway. No, he can do much better than that, in my honest opinion. I am speaking as your close friend, Edith."

"Anyway, no-one's going to look at him now, poor soul. He was no oil painting before the accident, bless him." She tried to laugh.

"He has beautiful eyes."

Edith studied her friend's serious face. "Yes he has."

"Not wishing to pry dear but a more mature woman would be better suited."

"I don't think…"

"Perhaps of independent means with a few sheckles behind her." The forced shrill laughter made Edith jump but noticed her friend's unblinking, grey eyes never left hers.

"I don't think he's given it that much thought."

Cynthia leaned closer. "We never know all their private thoughts, not even a mother does. Still waters run deep."

Edith looked into the grey eyes dancing with life. "Yes Cynthia, they do." None deeper than yours. "Help yourself to biscuits." Edith knew she was almost anorexic.

"Why not? A chocolate bourbon never killed anyone. I feel quite naughty dunking it in my tea," and they both laughed like school girls.

The late afternoon's drizzly rain murmured on the window's old glass and the light around them faded and softened.

Cynthia's long hair, fanning out onto her shoulders, white and stiff, seemed almost translucent, silhouetted against the window. She laid her prizefighter's hand on Edith's doll's hand. "My only concern is your well being dear. I do understand how you are feeling, I really do. Life can be a *ficking* bitch."

"Edith's eyebrows shot up and her gaping mouth muttered "Yes Cynthia, I agree, it can." She picked up the teapot. "I'll make us some fresh."

"The long white hair spun towards the water plopping from the cracked cast iron guttering outside the window. "Will it ever stop raining?"

CHAPTER SEVEN

It could have been the extra chocolate bourbon biscuit or her repressed feelings for a resurrected Egyptian mummy or the constant rain. Whatever the reason, Cynthia tripled her medication that night. She still had all her marbles. They just did not clink together any more. She had been planning this trip for some time and laid her head on the pillow.

At two minutes past midnight the mothball rocket blasted off towards the tip of the crescent moon. She had promised Stanley the trip of a lifetime. The putrid orange ape clung to her flowing white hair with an even wider grin on his excited face.

Edith's fidgety seven stones nudged the two hot water bottles around the bed. Lying on her side with knees drawn up, she listened to the muffled showers of rain splattering on the treeless street. She whispered a short prayer for Stanley, wondered how she would pay this week's rent and tried to ignore her panicking loneliness. She tugged on her snazzy red and white bed socks and draped a hot water bottle across her leg "Come on Edith, things are not that bad. It will be all right."

Stanley was happy with his new legs, although they still felt hot on the blackened silver seam where the welding torch had scorched his skin. He tipped pint after pint of beer down his throat but he was always thirsty. It did not make any sense.

He was sitting in a crowded theatre. The slick compere talked fast and loud. "Ladies and gentlemen, all the way from the Sierra, The Fabuloso Wiper Brothers."

To great applause, they pranced onto the stage, swishing and singing in perfect harmony. "Seven point eight, La, La, La, swish, swish, swish, seven point eight. La, La, La…" The rubber window wipers stared in terror at the blinding white spotlight.

Stanley yanked the steering wheel and was thrown upside down in his car seat onto the stage.

"Stand closer to the microphone friend. I think Stanley Kandle whatever deserves a big round of applause. All right Stanley, you know the rules. You take home everything you can remember. O.K. You have ten seconds, starting from NOW."

A forklift truck trundled onto the stage carrying 'Miss Bloody Gorgeous' in a baby doll negligee. She smiled and waved. Stanley waved back. Another truck carried a broken hearted divorcee. Another truck, a teenage single mother with her swarming brood. The procession speeded up. The Voluptuous, the Uninhibited, those seeking a real man, an older man, a naughty man, a tactile man.

What is Tack-Tile? He wondered. Good at D.I.Y.? Probably. Forget that one.

"Time's up Stanley, keep thinking, step closer to the microphone. Keep thinking. All right, you have one second, starting from NOW."

"The…Err…Err…The…"

"I'm sorry friend, we've ran out of time. A big round of applause for Stanley."

A thunderous crashing noise and screams followed. It was not the audience. Stanley could clearly see the women being buried alive under a growing pile of bricks by the grinning fork lift trucks. Seven point eight million bricks. "No… No." He clawed at the mountainous pile.

"That's the way the cookie crumbles. Say goodnight Stanley. Night everyone."

"No, get them out for God's sake." He screamed and his eyes jerked open.

"It's alright, it was just a bad dream. You're safe."

Unable to speak, unable to move, his terrified eyes pleaded with the nurse. What kind of bad dream am I in now?

Dominic switched off his phone. It was that time of the month for Lucy, which sent her a bit cuckoo. He was not afraid of her but better to keep a safe distance for a few days. He enjoyed the crowded insanity of Juno's, drinking shit green cocktails, hoarse and half deaf with loud talk and laughter over the concussive music.

He circled the perfumed young flesh, squeezed into tight nothings, gyrating under the delirious, thudding white lights. His dark eyes selected one. The music stopped.

"What's your name?" she asked.

"Sebastian" he smiled.

"I'm Sophie."

"I'm a test pilot. Fly prototype fighter jets mostly."

"Cool." She looked impressed.

The music restarted. On a scale of one to ten she was a 'ten' horny bitch. Barely eighteen, barely dressed, her face and body teased all kinds of promises. This would be easy. Later on he would show her a few things.

They drank more green shit and were sucked into the panting orgy of grinding bodies, tasting each other's sweat.

She pushed her body hard against his with her hands clasped behind his neck, moving up and down with slow thrusts. Jammed all together in the thunderous dancing mass of flickering lights her hand was suddenly inside his trousers.

He screwed up his eyes. "Yes, yes."

"Not yet." she laughed and slid her hand out of his trousers. "I have to go to the loo." She kissed him on the cheek and left. He limped back to the bar in a strange manner and leaned on it with crossed legs and crossed eyes, trying to ignore the aching bulge in his trousers. God, he was in agony.

Half an hour later she had still not returned. He could not believe it. The prick teasing bitch had ran out on him. He could not understand how she could resist him. She must be a fanny lover, a screaming pussy kisser. No other explanation. He could see her now, laughing with her fat arsed fanny friends. Well, it wasn't funny.

Tipsy new flesh rubbed up against him.

"Hi, I'm Sebastian."

"Hi, I'm Nicky."

They drank fresh green shit and danced.

Lucy flicked through 150 T.V. channels, smoked 20 cigarettes, drank 2 bottles of red wine to blot out the last 30 years and dreamed of wading through a million liquid gold coins to touch Dominic.

Dominic woke just before the dead hour of the night and saw Lucy's face. Nicky's hand aroused him. He gasped and Lucy disappeared with his new smile.

Sue repaired the smashed up faces of the alcoholic 'divers,' calmed the hysterical, treated the 'pill poppers' and 'vein shooters,' assisted in surgery and comforted all comers. Dominic was right, this place was a nuthouse but all the lunatics were outside. Relief was strong coffee and the grey early morning light on the windows. In the reflection was her mum sleeping in a chair next to the buried druids treasure.

Unstable as a split atom the lottery ticket glowed radio active pink in the dark silence of it's plastic coffin. A twitchy 8 million pound nuclear bomb, waiting to be exhumed by joyous fingers.

Sometime in the early hours, Stanley and Cynthia and the putrid orange ape collided on the fringes of the constellation of the *Great Bear.* Grainy footage was captured by an amateur astronomer.

The exhausted night crashed into a duck pond. The groggy survivors scrambled out and formed a queue outside Lucky Sid's surgery cradling two traumatised mallards. Normal service was resumed after a free frontal lobotomy.

Dead people don't dream so Stanley knew he was still alive.

The ducks pecked at the exposed nerve fibres in his punctured brain. His screaming only freaked them out.

CHAPTER EIGHT

Driving home, Sue had fallen out of love with nursing. The headaches and heartburn were nothing compared to the dalek's head lodged in the base of her spine. She had to tell someone about the ticket and what she should do but who could she trust? One of her many friends? Perhaps Lucy, she was family after all. Sleep first, then decide.

Dominic said goodbye to Nicky and promised to ring her later. He stood in the busy street with the hideous green mother of all hangovers. Where the hell was he? Did he really spend two weeks benefit money in one night? He knew one thing, he needed money, lots more money.

Sue swallowed a small brown painkiller to dissolve the dalek's head, two super strength paracetamol for her sledge hammered head and another painkiller for the pink ticket driving her bananas. She had to tell someone before going home. She stood outside a concrete block of flats, pressed the silver button and waited. A dead voice materialised in the horizontal slots. "Yes."

"Lucy, It's me, Sue."

A long silence followed, then "Come on up."

The flat was a mess and so was Lucy. "I have to talk to you about a big problem I have. It won't wait any longer."

Lucy's head, still reeling from last night's red wine and the early hour lit a cigarette with trembling hands. She would deny everything. What had Dominic told her sister?

She needed a drink. In the kitchen she tipped the dregs of wine into her coffee and sat down opposite her sister. Resigned to explaining why she was having an affair, her voice was shaky. "Just say what you have to say."

"Lucy, I don't want this to go any further."

Why was she so calm? "OK Sue, if that's what you want." How did she find out? They were so careful.

"I actually made the discovery a week ago."

Lucy's mind trampolined backwards but made no connection. She felt her face tightening up and remained silent.

"I've been agonising who to tell. It's ripping me apart. It is a very moral dilemma."

Lucy held her breath, looking at everything except her sister's face. "Who have you told?" She whispered.

"Well, strange as it may seem, no-one yet."

"I don't know what to say. I'm really sorry."

Puzzled by her sister's reply she continued. "Let me tell you the full story first."

Now Lucy looked bewildered. The full story? She needed another drink.

"Listen to this, you won't believe it. I found a winning lottery ticket."

Lucy stared open mouthed, unable to speak.

Sue leaned closer and dropped her voice. "It's worth, wait for it. Nearly eight million."

"Eight million." Lucy croaked, reshuffling her brain.

"Yes, I swear on mum's life, eight million."

Lucy tried to focus. Sue did not know about the affair. Her mouth stammered with incredulous relief. "Claim it Sue, for God sake claim it."

"Well, it's illegal and immoral. Then I think eight million, it's a lot of money. Set mum up. Set everybody up."

"How would anybody find out?"

"They wouldn't. The man who won it was in a car crash. He has retrograde amnesia. He can't remember anything that happened on the days before the accident."

The three litres of rainwater soaked up by Dominic on his long walk home diluted some of the green gunge in his head. His empty pockets added to his foul sober mood.

No sign of his wife. Good. He showered, changed clothes and dozed on the sofa.

"Morning Dominic."

His head jerked up. "Another car crash?"

"Pardon."

"Is that why you're late?"

"Is that supposed to be funny?"

"Only asking cherub."

She exhaled. "This is not normal Dominic."

"What, being married to you."

"Why did you marry me."

"Love, my sweet cherub. It was love, love. Pure, pure love."

"You're sad and sick, do you know that?"

"And you're a fat twat." He smiled at the rhyming slang. "Almost poetic cherub."

"A fat twat, am I?" The closest thing to hand was an unplugged ceramic table lamp.

50

She gripped it's base and hurled it in a 'kill shot.' It skimmed off the top of the sofa like a Dambuster's bouncing bomb and exploded on his raised arms.

He jumped up, scattering the shrapnel, rubbing his arm, fear in his eyes. "You crack brain twat." She looked around for another bomb. He saw his chance and escaped through the door. "Psycho bitch. I'm leaving you for good this time." The well practiced slamming of the front door followed. Sue collapsed on the sofa, exhausted.

Lucy picked up her phone. "Hello."

"Hi babe, I'm on my way over. Talk when I get there." Dominic's voice was patchy and breathless.

"Has Sue told…"

"Can't hear you, you're breaking up, speak soon."

Lucy floundered into the bathroom. God, she looked a mess. Sue must have told him. What happens now? Where's the bloody foundation? Eight million. Oh my God.

Sweaty anger dripped off Dominic's bug eyed face. The frantic cycle ride to Lucy's flat was a personal best. "That's it. I've told her I've had enough. You know what she called me the other day. *A twat's arsehole.* Now it's violence. I'm telling you, she's got a big shock coming." His out of breath rant left Lucy's surreal morning in warped overdrive.

"Dominic, listen to me. Has Sue told you about the lottery ticket?"

He looked at her like a confused bloodhound. "Lottery ticket?"

"She's found a winning lottery ticket. She came here earlier to tell you."

His confused eyes swivelled from side to side. "She's not said a word. Is it much?"

"Have a guess."

"A couple of hundred, who cares."

"You better sit down Dominic."

"I don't want to sit down."

Her pale blue eyes were close to his. "Eight million." It was barely a whisper.

Dominic's poleaxed body fell backwards into the armchair. "She's having you on."

"Why would she do that? Anyway, she swore on mum's life. She would never do that if it wasn't true. Why are you smiling?"

His panicking voice slobbered through his demented grin. "She's flipped, it's a sick joke. You don't know her like I do."

"All I can tell you Dominic is that I believe her."

His dark eyes widened. He pushed his hands through his long hair, bit his bottom lip and tapped his fingers on the armchair. He shook his head, the grin was gone.

"I've just fucked her off."

"My advice Dominic, is to unfuck her off."

Dominic leapt onto his flying machine. If the ride over was a personal best the return run on his silver torpedo broke the sound barrier.

Still breathing hard, he popped his head around the bedroom door. "Alright?"

Propped up in bed, Sue ignored him and continued watching the T.V.

He eased himself into the bedroom. "Sorry about earlier on. I'm a bit stressed at the moment. All this stupid quarrelling, pointless really."

"What do you want Dominic?" The words were clipped anger.

"All that silly shouting, just words, don't mean anything. Negative shit when you really think about it." He spread out his arms in submissive peace.

"Is it?" Her puffy eyes and blotchy face turned red.

"Well, yeah. Acting like children. Doesn't solve anything. Laughable really."

"All this is one big laugh, is that what you think?" A glaring squint paralysed him.

"No, no, of course not. What I mean is, lets get back to how things used to be. I'm still in love with that girl who walked down the aisle. What else matters?"

She returned his feeble grin. Her bloodshot eyes were moist now. "Dominic."

"Yeah." The feeble grin became a pathetic smile.

"Piss off."

He bit his lower lip with a tortured laugh. A gang of burly noughts formed a bodyguard around her bed. "Well, sleep on what I've said." He started to back out of the room. "I do worry about the crappy hours you have to work. I really do." She tuned up the T.V. volume. "Nothing you want to tell me then." The T.V. volume increased. His pearly teeth grated together as he closed the door with swearing breath.

He prowled through the house like a demented stalker. Where would she hide a lottery ticket? He pulled her handbag and purse inside out. He emptied drawers, cupboards, moved furniture, inspected vases, crockery, light fittings, the contents of the fridge-freezer. Looked behind wall prints, tipped books inside out. Removed soil from house plants. Every item in every room including the inside of the toilet cistern was dissected. If the ticket existed the fat bitch must have hidden it in the bedroom.

He whispered into his phone. "I've looked everywhere."

"She told me it's in the house. Just ask her." Lucy's annoyed whisper replied.

With everything back in place he paced the floor, waiting

for the shrill ringing from upstairs that would wake her for the nightshift. He felt knackered. His body jumped at the sound of the alarm clock and he flicked on the kettle.

"Cup of coffee?"

She groped her way out of the bed. "Feeling alright?"

"Just thought you would like one."

She sipped the coffee. "Something wrong Dominic? You seem agitated."

He took a deep breath. "Why didn't you tell me you found a winning lottery ticket."

I had to find out from Lucy."

She raised her eyebrows. "Lucy?"

"She phoned while you were sleeping. Kept going on about eight million."

"Coffee's nice."

"Don't fanny around. Just tell me what's going on. Is it true?"

"Attention seekers."

"What are you talking about?"

"Fat bitches like me. It's the kind of things we do when we are unhappy and desperate."

His mouth opened, closed and opened in gibberish *twalk*.

Sue showered and drank more strong coffee while Dominic sat and fumed. He would kill her. Just one more word, just one and he would swing for her. She sensed his dangerous mood and left without saying anything. The situation felt out of control.

His phone rang. "Yeah."

"Hi Dominic, it's Lucy. Sue has just phoned, she is claiming the money tomorrow morning. It's all true, I swear and I'm sure the ticket is still in the house…hello."

"I'm still here, I think. Speak to you later." His head felt like it had been chewed by a pit bull terrier for an hour and spat out. Had the fat bitch hidden it in the bedroom? The insane lust of finding £8,000,000 turned his dark eyes black.

A floorboard in the bedroom creaked under his laboured steps. His foot probed under the radiator. A loose board winced. He knelt down as if he was praying and ripped back the curled edges of the carpet. His fingers grappled with the short, loose board. He prised it out and peered into the dark gap between the joists.

He shoved his arm down the narrow gap. His hand wrestled with itchy insulation and something else. He tugged it all out onto the floorboards. The insulation was dirty and old but the plastic box looked new. His heart quickened. The ticket was inside, he was certain. He ripped the plastic lid off the buried treasure.

He stared into the box. It was empty.

Last night's dream regurgitated it's contents over Sue's unsuspecting eyes. The lottery ticket she cradled became a fattened baby. The innocent pink monster was a gorger of red blood cells. A lover of blood, a devourer of human flesh.

The X-rated horror movie was showing free repeat performances every night in vivid Technicolor.

Sue flicked open the purse and lifted out the pink lottery baby. It cooed and dribbled blood. She pushed it back inside the purse and snapped it shut. After several deep breaths she eased open the tarnished clasps again and stared inside. She had not imagined it. An almost invisible slit at the top, a hidden pocket. She prised it open and slid her fingers inside. A small black and white photograph, old and creased came out with her fingertips.

A young woman holding hands with a small boy smiled back at her. They were standing in front of a brick terraced house and seemed very happy. It was obvious they were mother and son. The timeless image of love held a special power. She slipped it carefully back into the purse.

She knew of course, who they were.

She walked to the end of the ward and stopped at Stanley's bed. He was sleeping. Sitting at his bedside was an elderly lady, eyes closed, hands locked together as if in prayer. She sensed someone's presence and opened her eyes.

Sue spoke "Is it Edith?"

"Yes."

Sue held out the photograph.

"Oh my God." Edith's hands covered her mouth and tears formed in her eyes. "Where did you get it from?"

"I found it inside this purse."

"Oh, I've not seen that for ages, or this." She smiled. "How young I was and Stanley…" The words choked away. "Thank you so much. Where did you find it?"

Sue looked at the sleeping 'mummy.' "I was behind Stanley when the lorry hit his car. The purse was lying in the road. This was also inside." She placed the lottery ticket in Edith's hand.

"Thank you. I'll check the numbers later, you never know."

"You don't have to Edith, it's a winning number."

"Ooohh, I'll take it down to the newsagents tomorrow morning."

"I don't think he'll give you the money."

"Why not?"

"Because it's nearly £8,000,000."

Dominic's phone rang. Before he could speak, Lucy's excited

voice garbled in his ear. "Turn on the local T.V. news, now. Quick or you'll miss it."

He dropped the phone and scrambled around for the T.V. remote.

"The missing lottery winner has come forward and claimed the £7,856,322. prize. It is a local lady, connected to the A&E Hospital, according to first reports. Looking ahead to the weather…" The news talk faded in his ears. He snatched up his phone and pressed his wife's number. "Damn." It was switched off. He called the hospital. She had already left. He heard tyres crunching on the gravel and ran outside.

He greeted his wife with loud laughter and open arms. "It's true then, I've just seen it on the news."

Sue locked her car door without looking up. "Yes it's true. I've given it back to the lady who won it."

He stopped laughing. "No more mind games. You've beaten me. Alright?"

"It's not mind games Dominic. It wasn't my ticket. I had a bad dream. The ticket would only bring bad luck." His insane stare made her step back.

"I don't believe you. Nobody would give up £8,000,000."

"I did." She unlocked the car.

"If you think you're keeping the whole lot, you better…"

She dived into the car and locked the doors. "It's gone Dominic. Don't you understand. I keep telling you, it would only bring bad luck."

He could not hear her. He was too busy kicking the front wing of her car as the spinning wheels reversed. Ga-ga Dominic chased the frightened vehicle down the drive, aiming more psychopathic kicks at the shrieking bodywork.

"£8,000,000 you fat, crack brain bitch, £8,000,000." His unhinged brain melted with each hysterical rant.

He stood alone in the driveway, panting with road rage, hands on his hips like Henry VIII, plotting to kill his wife. The car was gone and so was the money.

CHAPTER NINE

Stanley decided that no matter what happened he would stick it out to the end. He had come this far and was not giving up now. He was convinced *The Frogman and the Revenge of the Killer Jellyfish* was not the worst film he had ever seen.

The jarring music of a hundred piece orchestra played out the last unforgettable moments of the thrashing frogman. It took some time and it was a horrible way to go but the snorkelling madman deserved all he got.

Stanley changed his mind. It was the worst film he had ever seen. Two hours out of his life had been stolen but time was something he had plenty of.

After being submerged all those hours his skin felt cold and wrinkly. The stifling heat of the back garden buzzed with winged life. It felt good. He parked his wheelchair in the centre of the tropical sun and rolled sweet tobacco into a fat cigarette.

He wanted to run down the garden but that would be difficult with both legs amputated above the knee. The strange sensation of both legs still being intact left him peeping under the wheelchair blanket more than once. The sunny nicotine stroked his nerve endings and his head nodded in the hot air.

His brown eyes left their sockets and searched the street for his old friend, the Ford Sierra. He had forgotten *he* had been compressed into an undignified metal cube. Stanley hoped *he* would be reincarnated as a Jaguar Sports.

After a month in hospital he was gaunt, sore and tender. The least exertions left him light headed. He lifted his head towards the fevered sun and breathed in the fragrant white blossom. He had acquired the unenviable looks of a retired nineteenth century bare knuckle prizefighter, which was an improvement on a church roof gargoyle. Just.

He listened to the mating grunts of printed paper multiplying in the dark vaults of the bank. The soulless passion of eight million in an obscene Roman orgy. Money giving birth to money. It was almost incestuous.

Everything was different but nothing had changed. Except surviving the accident was more profound than winning all those millions. He had been spared. It was not his time to go yet. Other plans had been made for him. A second chance at life. But why? Perhaps a goddess was waiting for him further down the river.

"There you are Stanley love." Edith walked over to him. "Was the film any good?"

"If you like vinegar on your jellied eels."

She looked concerned. "Don't stay out in the sun too long."

"It's hotter in Australia."

"Yes but we still have an ozone layer to stop us getting fried. Anyway the man on the telly reckons Antarctica is melting and to expect a tidal wave down the street any day now." She made a dramatic sweeping motion with her hand.

He couldn't beat that one and rolled more tobacco between his fingers.

"I'm so glad this house belongs to us now." She gazed at the brick terrace. "I really do love it here. I don't think I could leave it. Could you Stanley?"

The old brickwork and roof sagged in the day's heat. "I could be persuaded."

She ignored him. "No more bills to worry about. Isn't life wonderful and no more working in that horrible brickyard."

Diesel fumes filled his nostrils. The forklift truck eyeballed him. Pallets of bricks danced with mad glee in front of his brown eyed stare. He felt dormant spots bubbling under his skin. No more shift work. No more early morning alarm calls. No more legs.

Still, here he was. The sun on his face and millions in the bank. Back from the dead. A jim-dandy lunatic's dream.

"Yes mum, you're right, life is wonderful."

Sitting outside in his wheelchair, his body became a sacrificial burnt offering to the sun god of early summer. Time seemed to pass slower. All the insects seemed to move faster. The sun ironed out the car crash dents in his skull. The flowering plants breathed out scented oxygen into the hothouse garden. Their fragrance and the birdsong lullabies sucked the near death crash from his brain.

He squinted upwards. A jet rumbled across the cloudless blue sky. Expanding white vapour trailed behind the glittering silver as it crept by the sleeping ghost of the moon. In the hot silence of the long narrow garden he fell asleep.

Stanley's open mouthed snoring in the afternoon sun was disturbing no-one when a petrol mowing tsunami smashed into his dreaming brain. He was a soft target for that kind of terrorism. Enraged, he snatched up his phone and punched in the numbers of the American C.I.A.

"Err, hello, I'd like to hire a drone for the day."

"Yes sir-ree. Is this an exercise or this real time."

"Err, this is real time and I'm a big lottery winner."

"O.K. buddy, shouldn't be a problem. Just getting the authorization. O.K. Yeah, I 10-4 that. It's a go. Scramble XDX. Target to be confirmed."

"Excuse me, err…good buddy, is that a drone for the whole day?"

"Yes sir, we don't believe in pissing into the wind."

"Err, yes…Well, thank you good buddy and err…over and out."

"Nice speaking with you sir."

As the phones clicked off a classified shitload of dollar bills changed hands and the son-of-a-bitch drone was on it's goddamn way.

The mid-life crisis bloke, three gardens away, who mowed his nine square yards of lawn with an ear splitting, industrial, sit on mower was in for a big surprise.

Silent and invisible, the drone approached the English coastline from the South West, 40,000 feet above the earth's surface. The computerised pre-historic creature swooped out of the sun, hungry eyes locked on the tasty meal below.

The terrorist petrol mower, deep inside it's wooden lair was already planning another outrage for Sunday afternoon. Stanley was guaranteed to be asleep in his garden at that time.

It was vaporised mid rotor blade cackle by a *Flash Gordon* gamma ray. Stanley waved at the *The Thing From Mars* as it performed a victory roll over the rooftops, clipping several T.V. ariels.

Stanley nodded, that's what money can do. It can solve problems. Take away the things in life you don't like or agree with. It was a revelation. Forget shiny baubles, money had power and control over life and death. A visionary futurist.

The enlightened Stanley went back to sleep.

"Dare I ask, how are we today?"

Stanley turned his head towards Cynthia's precise vowels. The glare from her yellow and blue and orange flowery dress began to melt his sunglasses.

"He's feeling much better." Edith fussed around him. "Getting back to his old self."

Stanley's stuttering reply faded.

"That is good news, but one must be careful of exposing one's self too long in the sun."

He raised his eyebrows. 'Exposing myself.'

"I suppose the vitamin D in natural sunlight is beneficial. It has certainly put some colour back into his cheeks."

"You are going a bit pinky red love." Edith touched his boiling skin.

He tried to focus on his cigarette rolling through the pulsating yellow and blue and orange strobe lights.

"I find this an absolute lifesaver dear." Her arm swung over the garden fence like a giant crane on a building site.

"Look at this love, factor fifty sun cream. Thank you Cynthia. Isn't that kind Stanley." Before he could say 'factor off' the 'life saver' was being smeared over his face. "Please keep still love."

"One could easily faint in this heat. Then I would have to give you mouth to mouth resuscitation Stanley." Cynthia's shrill laughter almost lifted the sun cream off his face. The tobacco jumped out of his startled fingers.

Edith joined in. "Oh, I think he'd rather enjoy that, wouldn't you love." He tried to roll fresh tobacco while whistling a flat tune.

"I do so pray it rains soon, the gardens are parched. Must fly, I have a man coming to creosote the fence. Bye everyone."

"Bye Cynthia." Edith waved. Stanley grunted. She smeared fresh white cream over his burning skeletal body. "She always asks after you."

"That's the one I like. I really fancy that."

She looked down at the colour magazine centrefold. "What is it?"

"A large Edwardian house sitting in an acre of landscaped gardens."

"A bit isolated for me. We wouldn't have neighbours like Cynthia."

He grimaced. "No mum, we wouldn't."

She pinched his arm. "Stanley, be nice. I'll make us a nice cuppa."

At last he managed to light his 'roll up' and exhaled a deep drag of thin smoke. The sun continued to burn the hot pinky skin stretched over the reclining skeleton and his satellite dish ears glowed transparent red.

A pair of magpies called to each other in that piercing, unsettling sound like rattling bursts of a World War 1 machine gun. Probably something after their eggs he thought.

The frenzied Roman orgy licked the wax in his ears. He smiled and dozed in the new enforced silence of greenhouse heat.

CHAPTER TEN

The eight million silver bullet head shot would have killed most men but Dominic was not 'most men.' The fat, stupid bitch should have known that. His progression from a staggering wreck to a shuffling wreck to walking without crutches was miraculous. He was back.

A new red and silver flying machine, courtesy of the taxpayer, simmered on it's launch pad.

"So, when *are* you telling her?" Lucy was nervous.

"In the morning babe."

"Are you sure it's what you want.?"

"Yeah, I'll show her."

"She'll never talk to me again. She'll hate me."

"Don't let it bother you."

"Well it does, she is my sister."

"A bit late for that now. Look, we've talked it through enough times. If we want to be together, this is the only way."

"Alright Dominic, so long as you love me."

"Yeah, of course babe. Just you and me." He kissed her and knocked back some blue shit from a weird shaped bottle. She lit another cigarette knowing that his one and only true love was himself.

Dominic's new flying machine seemed faster than the previous silver torpedo or was it a new peak of fitness? It would not surprise him. He felt nervous about the confrontation with his wife. Perhaps he should phone her instead.

He rode up to their house. No car on the drive. He felt overwhelming relief and hurried around inside, stuffing socks, underpants and shirts into his rucksack. Time to get out of here, pick the rest up later.

"Did you tell her?" Lucy was on her tenth cigarette of the morning.

"No, she wasn't there. I waited ages. I'll tell her when I get the rest of my stuff."

"You seem very calm about everything,"

"Yeah, that's me babe, Mr cool. I'll give her the good news tonight, face to face."

When evening came he waited until she had started a new shift and ordered a taxi. Probably best to tell her over the phone. Anyway it made no sense to remove all his clothes first. He was so relieved again when there was no sign of her car.

"Was she there?"

"No, I missed her again. I'll sort it out."

Lucy stared at the pile of suitcases. "How many clothes have you got?"

"This is not all of them."

"Dominic, this is a one bedroom flat, there is no space for them."

"Don't worry, I need a drink."

"So do I."

Two hours later he punched in his wife's number and waited.

"Dominic, where the bloody hell are you?"

"Never mind about that, I've got something to tell you." He had another gulp of yellow shit and burped. "Are you there?"

"Yes I'm here, what's wrong?"

"I've had enough…of you…of the…Of everything."

"You're slurring your words, are you drunk?"

"I'm trying to tell you I've had enough. Do you get it?"

"If it's about the lottery ticket I…"

"Ah, yeah, the lottery ticket. I'd almost forgotten about that."

"I tried to tell you. I had a bad dream about it. The ticket would only bring bad luck to the person who…"

"Bad luck. What do think I've had for the last year since I married you."

"Look, it's a busy night. I've got to go. I don't want a slanging match now. I'll talk to you in the morning."

"Hold on, hold your horses. I won't be there in the morning."

"Why not?"

"Because my love, I'm leaving you."

Sue tried to reply but the words were lost in her panicking disbelief.

"Nothing to say. Good. Enjoy the rest of your life fatso. I'm gone."

The phone went dead. She reeled backwards in shock. The tears would come later.

The dream still tormented Sue and the more she thought about it, the more convinced she became. The ticket was bad luck or something worse. Stanley had won it and nearly died the same day. She had found it and now her husband had left her.

She was lying in bed at midday on sick leave, two days after Dominic had walked out. She still could not believe he had done it over the phone. Where was he sleeping? She felt lousy. Her phone rang.

"Hello Sue, it's Stanley. I hope it's convenient to talk."

"Hello Stanley." How strange when she was just thinking about him.

"Mum and I think it's only right to make you a millionaire. Well, a double millionaire in fact. Everything's in place with the bank and the solicitor's. Just need a couple of your signatures and your bank details and the two million is yours. Hello…"

The headache, the backache and every other ache stampeded into her throat and became lodged. She gasped. "Can I phone you back Stanley."

"Yes, of course, hope it's not too much of a shock."

She covered her face with both hands. "Oh my God."

Lucy's phone rang. "Hello."

"Hi Lucy, it's Sue…Hello, can you hear me?"

"She held her breath and gulped. "Hi Sue."

"I don't know where to start. Dominic walked out on me two days ago and now the

Lottery ticket winner is giving me, wait for it, two million as a reward."

"Two million." Lucy croaked. She tried to clear her head. "Do you know where Dominic is?"

"No, the bastard told me over the phone. He'll soon be back when he hears about this."

"Would you have him back?"

"I want it all to work out, I really do but he's such a cold bastard."

"I wouldn't tell him about the money for obvious reasons."

"Yes, you're probably right. He's not answering my calls anyway. Once I get the money I'll see you and mum are set up. I'll speak to you soon. Right now I need a strong drink. Bye for now."

"Bye Sue, take care."

"Who were you on the phone to?" Dominic had walked into the bedroom.

"Sue. She wants to know where you are."

"I could phone her later on I suppose."

"No. Leave it for a few weeks." She would lose him if he knew about the money.

He looked relieved. "Are you sure, I thought we had agreed to…"

"No rush Dominic. Do you promise not to tell her?"

"Yeah, I promise. Did she say anything else?" His puzzled face enquired.

"No, that's it. Right now I need your hot cock."

One week later.

"Hi Lucy, it's Sue, I'm phoning from Florida. I just needed to get away."

"Florida, fantastic, I don't blame you." The further away the better, Lucy thought.

"Can you do me a favour. Pick up some photos from the chemists and take them to Stanley and Edith's house, 97 Albert Street. It's snaps of them and myself together in their beautiful garden. I thought it would be nice if you could take them over. They are expecting you."

"Yes, of course I can. This is the lottery winners?"

"Yes, they are lovely people. I've told them all about you and warned Stanley the bachelor to be on his guard." The laughter faded. "Have you heard from Dominic?"

"No, nothing at all. When are you coming back?"

"A couple of weeks maybe. I'll call you before I do. I need time to think."

"Alright, have fun, I'll see you when you return." Lucy's smile made her jaw ache. Things could not have worked out better and now she was meeting a millionaire.

The long days of sun in the shadeless back garden had burnt and blistered his loose pink skin until it was toasted to a rich, crinkled brown. His newly shaven head, silver earrings and black sunglasses gave him the look of a villain, back from an extended stay in 'The Costa's.'

He sat in his wheelchair in the day's new heat among the flowering white blossoms on the green lawn, sipping fresh tea and rolling fresh tobacco. The garden was alive with birds and insects. Sweat dripped off him. His drowsy eyes watched frenzied ants swarming over his discarded apple core.

"Stanley love, we have company. A young lady to see you." His mum's voice was carried on the hot air down the garden. A young lady? He didn't know any.

Soft curves sauntered towards him on four inch white stilettos, breasts nudging against a loose fitting pale green blouse. Dark shades, dark smiling lips, creamy combed back hair. It was hard to breathe.

"Hi, I'm Lucy, Sue's sister." Her voice, roughened by her twenty a day habit, had the same fascination as her face and body. "Sue asked me to drop these photos off to you." She looked around. "I love your garden, it's beautiful." Flattery always pays.

"Yes, thanks." Behind his sunglasses his eyes tried to lick every inch of her. "It's all mum's work. She's got the touch with flowers and plants."

"It's really lovely. I can't grow anything." She glanced around the garden again. "Well, I'll leave you in peace to enjoy it."

He stopped licking her and started to panic. "Err…stay and have a cuppa, unless you have to be somewhere." He held his breath. He would beg her to stay.

"No. I mean I don't have to leave yet." Her smile caressed his aching tongue.

He breathed out. "I'll tell mum to make a fresh pot." He followed the supple movements of her body with the jerking movements of his wheelchair back to the steamy cooking smells of the claustrophobic kitchen.

"Go on through to the dining room love." Edith sang out. After the glare of the garden sun the back room was gloomy and cold. Wax polish and stale tobacco clung to the hybrid of scarred wooden chairs and stringy armchairs jostling for position around the red Formica table. Doors had been removed for wheelchair access and the doorframes had deep gouges from Stanley's chariot wheels.

An elongated head jumped out of the gloom. She stepped back from the startling apparition. It was her own distorted refection from a circular convex mirror. Perhaps it was her real face. It was how she felt most of the time. She spun around with fright again as Stanley's wheelchair careered into the room, splintering the doorframe, leaving fresh chariot wheel gouges. Edith followed him in with chocolate digestives and tea. "Take your time Stanley love, there won't be a house left at this rate."

Lucy was almost tempted by the table centrepiece. A

chipped white bowl of ripened porcelain fruit, deliciously painted and begging to be eaten.

A pair of large bluebottles zoomed around their heads, dodging the wild swings of Edith's newspaper cudgel, before bouncing off the window and zooming over their heads again. Lucy ducked under Edith's delayed fresh air swipes. If she had thought she had fallen down a rabbit hole it was confirmed when Cynthia materialised next to her in a green and orange dress that mimicked the whirling carpet.

"Oh Cynthia, you do brighten up a room."

"Thank you Edith." Her grey eyes summed up her tarty rival. The sugary vinegar Lucy. Gathered around the red Formica table, the mad hatter's tea party began with the dunking of digestives and inane chatter. After a while Edith suggested to Cynthia they sit outside in the garden. Cynthia reluctantly left Stanley alone with the tart.

He gave her a strange forced smile in the gloomy nervous silence. She smiled back. Sue had told him Lucy had no boyfriend at the moment. He took a deep breath. "There's a lovely park nearby." His sudden rapid blurt made her jump and his hesitant voice tailed off. "I wonder if you'd like to go there with me sometime?"

Her pale blue eyes inched closer to his twitching face. "Yes, I would love to."

His Mediterranean garden tan crumpled into a bright smile. "Err…what about tomorrow…err…midday, at the front gates?" He stuttered. "If you're free."

"Yes, midday is perfect Stanley."

His smile grew wider. Hearing her say his name left him wanting more, much more.

She smiled back at him again and glanced casually around the room. It was hard to believe he was a multi millionaire.

He had not spent a penny, on anything. It was all sitting in the bank. All those millions. What a delicious thought.

On the roasting bus ride home, she could not stop thinking about the giddy amounts of money. It left her giggly and light headed like a teenage love thing. He liked her, she could tell. What if…? No. Why not? Access to millions of pounds was like… There was no comparison. It was hard to control the trembling excitement rising from her tummy. She needed a drink.

"What did you think of her mum?"

"Seemed very nice Stanley. Very pretty. Yes, I liked her."

"Good. I'm meeting her down the park tomorrow. Try out the new buggy."

"Oh you dark horse. You don't waste any time do you. It will do you good, get out of the house for a bit."

"What did Cynthia think of her?"

Edith smiled. "Not much."

"Dominic, what is that thing hanging on my wall?"

"Do you like it?"

"No I don't. What's it supposed to be?"

"I'll give you a clue." He stood next to the large abstract painting with a stupid grin on his face.

"A naked posing prat with a big cock would be my guess."

"You're half right babe."

"What, the posing prat bit?"

"Yeah, you know." He stood back from the four foot high masterpiece, nodding in admiration. "Three sittings, wasn't cheap."

"Dominic, it's not staying. I'm not looking at that every morning over my cornflakes."

"Give it time. You must admit, it does have a mythical

beauty about it." The intense stare of his glazed eyes was a schoolboy's mad crush.

She left him alone with his new love and thought about hers.

CHAPTER ELEVEN

It was another cloudless day. Stanley's mobility scooter purred through the wide entrance to the park and stopped just inside. He was early. The Victorian spiked railings and ornate, swirling gates, warmed by the hot morning sun, were thick with the smell of fresh black paint.

He looked across the expanse of freshly mown grass surrounded by high trimmed hedges and rustling trees, heavy with new leaves. Glistening water rainbows arced over banks of vibrant flowers. Distant squealing laughter floated towards him. Every day was better than the last. He breathed it all in.

"Where are you going?"

"The usual, just round the charity shops and coffee." Lucy was dressed for a killing.

"You gone to a lot of trouble for a charity shop."

"You never know who you'll bump into. I think the painting looks better today."

"Told you it would grow on you. Depends how the light catches it. I swear it changes colour." He walked over to it and sighed. Lost in it's pulsing, surreal reflection, Dominic never heard the door close.

The jolting bus journey did not help Lucy's cart-wheeling

brain. Not telling Dominic about meeting a middle aged man in a park, who she hardly knew, could seem strange, but living with Dominic was stranger. It was not how she imagined it would be. His untidiness, dominating the T.V. remote and making the bathroom stink were just starters. A daily orgasm help balance it up.

After years of nothing, her life was now an exciting, highly addictive game. The more she thought about the £6000,000 the more she could not *stop* thinking about it.

Stanley had an irresistible urge to run across the extensive lawns. He thumped his stumps in frustration and winced, tears in his eyes. His newly shaven head gleamed with sweat. She was fifteen minutes late, he would give her another…

"Hello Stanley."

His heart and stomach tightened. The soft husk of a voice was instantly recognisable. He spun his scooter around. He would not have believed she could look any better than yesterday but she did. White sleeveless blouse tucked into tight ice blue jeans. Dark sunglasses, smiling lilac lips in a creamy complexion, slicked back creamy hair. A five and a half foot beauty.

He almost swallowed his words. "Morning Lucy."

The short, hot shadows of the midday sun moved side by side with the beauty and the beast as they crossed the open green space, breathing in the freshly cut grass. They stopped at a shady park bench. He offered her a 'roll up' from a large circular tin. She shook her head with a smile and lit one of her own.

"We share at least one bad habit then." She smiled again.

"There is worse." He drank her in from behind his sunglasses. "Tell me to mind my own business but do you have a boyfriend or…"

She looked up and blew whispers of smoke into the clear blue sky. "No, I don't mind you asking and no, I don't have a boyfriend, at the moment."

He tried not to jump up and down but fidgeted in his wheelchair, searching for his matches. "I thought you would have."

"Just haven't found the right man yet, to commit to. I suppose it would be nice, I am pushing thirty."

"Thirty, that's no age, I'm fifty and still single." A pathetic laugh followed.

"Fifty is a good age for a man. He's matured, sowed all his wild oats."

Wild oats? He wouldn't know one if it smashed him over the head. "Yes, perhaps you're right but who would look twice at *me* now?"

"You would be surprised Stanley." Her dark sunglasses gave nothing away. The upturned corners of her mouth teased.

He fished around in his tin for another 'roll up.' "Are you working at the moment?"

"In between jobs as they say. Nearly all my time is taken up with voluntary charity work, through the church and other organisations." She crossed her fingers and toes.

He pawed his shaven head in thought. "You make me feel guilty. I should be doing something like that instead of just sitting around every day."

"Oh I'm sure you will, when you are feeling up to it again."

"Yes." He rubbed his stumps. At odd moments he forgot his legs were gone. That peculiar sensation of still feeling them repeated it's cruel joke on his brittle mind. They talked and smoked for an hour. He wanted to know everything about her and the more he knew, the more he wanted.

She knew it was time to go by the fluttery twinges inside her head. Her fingers touched the small bottle tucked in her handbag. "Well Stanley, it's been really lovely but duty calls. Afternoon meals to deliver to the housebound."

"Yes, of course. I feel guilty again, taking up your time."

"Don't be silly, I've really enjoyed your company." She stood up to leave.

Panicking, he blurted out "Perhaps we could meet again, later in the week."

She hesitated. "It's a bit tricky. Friday, I could make, midday again."

He breathed out. "Friday, at the main gates." It was an almost breathless reply.

She bent over and kissed him on the cheek. "I'll put you in my diary." With a smile she left the cool shadows of the trees and walked into the bright sunshine. A little wave over her shoulder made his heart jump. His creased, smiling face watched the adorable creature, white against the green foliage, grow smaller and disappear through the gates. She was gone. He felt panic spasms again.

This was ridiculous, feeling like this. He had only known her since… Yesterday? What was the matter with him? He knew he was in trouble. He was all over the place.

Lucy sat at the back of the near empty bus on the journey home. She was feeling good and the hurried swigs from the small bottle made everything better than good. The perverse excitement every day had trampled over her previous drab existence. She was alive. Stanley liked her. The golden multi-million key to eternal pleasures had left an indentation in her hand. *Lucy's Key.* She liked the sound of that.

"Dominic, what is that?"

"My new ring tone. Like it?"

"No, it sounds ridiculous."

"Everybody loves Hawaii Five -O."

"I don't."

Lucy left him straddling the arm of the sofa, rowing with an imaginary paddle, belting out the theme tune. "Ba ba ba ba bar bar, ba ba ba ba bar."

She shouted through the bedroom door. "Where did this come from?"

He continued paddling. "It's the mirror from my house. I need it for workouts and things. Looks good. What do you think?"

"It's too big for the room."

"I need it babe." He continued paddling through the crazy surf, singing the crazy theme tune.

She shrugged her shoulders and undone the buttons on her blouse. It fell to the floor. She peeled off the ice blue jeans and eased down her panties. A soft breeze from the window stroked her naked body. She sprinkled lavender over her skin and posed in the mirror. She was still a horny bitch.

"Dominic."

"Yeah."

"I need your cock. *Now.*"

"Book 'em Dano." He paddled towards the bedroom door with renewed energy.

CHAPTER TWELVE

The sweltering summer days melted together. Stanley was awakened early Friday morning by the nervous excitement of seeing Lucy in the coming hours. When he drifted back to sleep shooting pains in his stubs jarred him upright in bed. Perhaps they were in a state of re-growth.

His chariot wheels left new splintered gouges in the outside doorframe on the way to his morning sabbatical. In the tranquilised hush of the back garden he watched the thin morning mist evaporate into the sharp brightness of a new day. It left a fresh dampness on his face. He listened to the garden breathing out and sucked in it's sweet, pure air.

Breakfast was a brace of brown painkillers, a fattened strong 'roll up' and stronger dark coffee, laced with white sugar and evaporated milk.

His born again brain tried to imagine what he would be doing now at the start of a new shift. Tearing around the brickyard with all the other poor sods on their doolally forklifts, loading the first 10,000 bricks of the day.

Money had given him freedom. He had bought it like an ancient slave might have. Freedom, it was a powerful thing and so was money. One gave birth to the other.

The shooting pains eased as the brown pills kicked in and

his thoughts shuttled over to Lucy. Getting her out of his head was becoming a problem. Never seeing her again frightened him. Would she be showing all this interest in him if he was driving a forklift? He'd like to think so.

He relit his 'roll up.' Who was he kidding? The truth was he didn't care. He only knew he had to see her again. Reason, Justification? They had no place in his feelings for her.

The painkillers made him drowsy and his head nodded in a hot sun now buzzing with insects. The besotted Quasimodo dreamed of the beauty stroking his fiery stubs with her cool white hands. She did not disappoint him.

"You look smart Stanley love." Edith fussed around him.

"Meeting Lucy down the park again."

"Ooohh, getting serious."

"Don't be daft. She's good company. We get on well and…"

"I'm surprised she's not with anyone."

"Yes, so am I."

"A young, attractive girl like that. Is she divorced or anything?"

"Anything?" He shook his head. "I don't know mum. You've met her. She's just a nice easy person to talk to and she does all kinds of charity work through the church. Does that put your mind at rest?"

"Only asking love, no need to get shirty. She seems quite a catch then."

"Yes, I suppose she is." His reply was quiet and almost dreamy.

"I'll make you a little picnic. I picked up some fresh haslet from the butcher's yesterday. I know how much you like it."

"I've been meaning to have a word with you about…"

"I'm off down the Co-op in a bit." She held up a

newspaper advert. "Half price custard creams and ginger snaps. Some wonderful bargains this week."

"Mum, you don't have to shop for bargains any more. We have six million in the bank. The interest alone could buy a third world country."

"But they are half price Stanley."

He wondered if she had caught 'Forklift Fever.' "I forgot to tell you. I've gave Mr Jamal money for another shop, it's what he always talked about."

"Very good of you Stanley. It's the least we could do for holding on to the ticket. I'll leave your 'haslet picnic' near the door." She kissed him on the forehead. "Just be careful, parks can be dangerous places."

Stanley positioned himself in the cool shadows of the old trees, close to the black spiked railings at the park entrance. He was early again.

He had just watched a desperate woman having a complete makeover on T.V. costing £40,000. So he estimated he would get no change from £100,000 for his 'renovation.' If he was lucky.

It had only cost him two hours out of his life for his makeover but was time now more precious than money? Perhaps, but time could not buy his freedom. Time destroys it. The two hours was still a great investment and success except for the hairs plucked from under his nose, enough for a toupee and had left him reaching for the painkillers. The area was now a spreading red blotch.

His shaven head, white teeth and ironed white shirt all gleamed. Saturated in *Eau Du Toilette* and talcum powder he peered through the iron railings like a condemned man. She was late again. What if she did not come this time? He did not have her telephone number. Idiot. Sadness drained him. He slumped in his wheelchair.

"Hello Stanley." The husk of a voice overwhelmed him with joyous relief. He looked up and gaped at the bare legged beauty in brief yellow flowered shorts and matching heeled sandals. Her pale yellow top rippled in the warm breeze.

She smiled back at his open mouthed gawp with deep pink lips he hoped would devour him. The black sunglasses and creamy slicked back hair completed the fantasy.

He was a long way down the river before this moment and now…

She shimmered closer. Fresh sweat mingled with his *Eau Du Toilette*. The delicious fragrance of her body leaned over him and she kissed him on the cheek with moist lips

Stanley disappeared over the edge of the waterfall. His mum was right, parks can be dangerous places.

"You're looking very handsome today Stanley."

"Lovely, just lovely" he whispered. It was obviously illegal to look the way she did. She must have caused at least a couple of 'pile ups' crossing the roads.

His eyes ached at sideway glances through his sunglasses at her quivering flesh as they crossed the expanse of grass to 'their' shady park bench. He inched as close as he dare to her bare crossed legs. "Did you manage all your deliveries?"

"Deliveries? Oh those. Yes, they all had their meals."

"It must be very satisfying."

That afternoon riding Dominic's big cock popped into her head. "Yes it was." She smiled, the image was hard to remove. "So, how have you been?"

He drew hard on his 'roll up.' "Just grateful to be alive." Behind his sunglasses his eyes wandered up and down the curves of her crossed bare legs.

"Well I'm grateful you're alive."

"Really?"

"I'm very fond of you Stanley."

"Oh." His heart and mouth stalled. "Really?"

"Still, I suppose with your money you could have the pick of the ladies. A man in demand. Think about it."

"I have." His sunburnt features crumpled into his gargoyle grin. "Gold diggers, plenty of them out there. No. One decent woman, I'll be happy with that."

"I see what you mean. Yes, it would be easy to attract the wrong sort." It was an Oscar nominated face.

He looked at her, half smiling. "You and your sister are so different."

She half smiled back and put her sunglasses on. How could he know? What had he found out about her and Miss Goodey Two Shoes? She held her breath and waited.

"What I mean is, you are both so different from other women I've met."

"In what way?"

"In the nicest possible way. Honest and genuine."

She blinked and breathed out with relief. "Very sweet of you to say so Stanley."

"It's the truth."

"So, one decent woman. When you find her, what then?"

"Oh, she would have to adapt to my set ways, wouldn't be easy for her." His face creased up again with a smile.

"I'm sure." She leaned towards him. "You have dropped some ash on your lap." She brushed it off with little flicks and slow sweeps of her fingers. "Is that better?"

Staring at her hand still resting over his zip he gulped "Yes."

She had never seduced anyone in a wheelchair before. It was a new experience. She liked it. So did Stanley. It could be fun, a kind of bondage game. Control and power over him. Doing what she did best, making him beg, driving him crazy. It had great appeal, playing the dominant slut. He would love it. Any man would.

"You don't want hot ash on it, do you?"

He gulped again. "What?"

"Your trousers." Her pale blue eyes were very close to his. "A decent woman you say. Would I have a chance?" Her hand over his zip moved from side to side.

If he had been pelted with a bushel of wild brussel sprouts he could not have been more gob-smacked. "Err, yes, I mean more than a chance. I was hoping…"

She lifted her hand from his zip and placed her fingertips on his lips. "I think we both feel the same Stanley. You are the most wonderful human being."

He gripped her hand with his large, crooked paw. If she asked him now to get out of his wheelchair and run three times around the park bench he would. "I've dreamed of this. It's unbelievable."

"Ah bless. You're shaking like a leaf, poor love. Come here."

Embraced in her cool perfumed flesh under the dappled shade of the park's great oaks the resurrection of Stanley was complete.

Lucy sat on the back seat of the empty bus celebrating with constant sips from a new quart bottle, Her face and body, fanned by a hot breeze from the open windows, swayed with the motions of the bus as it lurched from street to street.

She had promised to see Stanley at his house tomorrow afternoon. The old girl's blessing was vital. Things were moving at a pace. Stay with Dominic for now, keep all her options open. Sue was staying longer in Florida, which simplified things. Yes, everything was perfect and yes, anything was possible. She licked the inside of the empty bottle.

CHAPTER THIRTEEN

"You're always going somewhere, it's getting on my tits and I'm starving. Can't you do me a meal, knock something up?"

"Dominic, I don't do cooking. Get something from the fridge." Lucy was in a hurry.

"There's nothing in the fridge."

"Then buy something to put in the fridge. You'll find it in a supermarket. They ask for pennies which you get from a bank. Think you can do that without me holding your hand?"

"You're becoming a right comical twat lately, do you know that."

"Runs in the family sweetie. I shan't be long."

"Don't I know it. Anyway, where are you going?"

"Unlike you Dominic I have friends to socialize with."

"I've got friends you cheeky bitch."

"See you later Tarzan boy. Don't pine for me too much. I'll give you some hot fanny later if you're good. Byee."

Dominic's habit of wandering around the flat naked was a throwback to the 'let it all hang out *man*' culture of the 1960's. He was a reconstituted flower child. A 25th century barbwire hippie.

His sublime reflection in the full length mirror pleased

him. He postured and posed, each one more beautiful than the last. His eyes studied every straining muscle, every taut, perfect curve. Lucy would get a good shafting tonight, lucky bitch. He almost wished he could take her place.

He strutted into the lounge and stood in front of his abstract portrait. As always it took his breath away. He felt aroused. It should really be hanging in an art gallery. The world needed to see this beautiful 'Michelangelo's David.'

Lucy was smartly dressed for the visit to Stanley's house. A good impression on the old girl was absolutely vital. She needed Edith's blessing or she could lose Stanley. She believed they were that close. A botched hacking at the umbilical cord could leave a very bloody mess.

"Lucy's here Stanley." Edith voice carried down the garden. She returned to her guest. "Kettle's on love. I've got some lovely vanilla slices made with fresh cream. Stanley's favourite." Lucy's reply was lost in a fresh splintering of wood on the abused doorframe from the charioteer's wheels.

"Look out, Ben-Hur's in town" Edith called out.

In the dining room Stanley's face beamed at Lucy across the red Formica table. She half beamed back. "You look great." he whispered. Her dark blue top and skirt, soft pink lipstick, minimal make-up and no jewellery emphasised 'the girl next door' look. Her pale blue eyes softened, moist with a naïve chastity.

Edith scuttled in, removed the delicious bowl of untouched porcelain fruit and replaced it with a silver tiered cake stand. Balanced on it's four levels were vanilla slices and long creamy doughnuts. "Leave one for the rest of us Stanley. He's terrible with fancy cakes."

"We don't have them that often."

"Ooohh, he's a terrible liar as well." She poured steaming black tea through a silver tea strainer into white china cups bursting with red climbing roses. "It's lovely to see you again Lucy. Stanley's told me about your picnics in the park."

Picnics? Lucy looked puzzled. "Yes, it's such a peaceful place to sit and talk and they keep it so lovely."

"Oh, I agree, he's certainly perked up since his visits there with you. Done him the world of good. Cake nice love?" He nodded through his packed vanilla slice smile.

Lucy nibbled at a doughnut. "I would like to spend more time together but it's just fitting it in around all my charity and voluntary work."

"Now you are making us feel guilty." She looked at her son , still incapacitated by the cake. "Once he's back to his old self we'll look into charity donations but it must be hard, working all those hours."

"I have to be honest and say it I don't look upon it as work. I enjoy it and it's very rewarding. I suppose it's the same for you Edith, when you are working in your garden to keep it looking so beautiful."

"Bless you. Did you hear that Stanley? What an angel you are."

Lucy sipped the unusually thick tea without flinching. "Lovely brew Edith." she smiled. Anything that was necessary.

The afternoon chit-chat crossed over into the evening. Fresh tea was mashed, fresh 'Iced Fancies' served up. It grew darker outside, a thunderstorm threatened. Lamps were switched on. The room glowed.

"Well Edith, it's been really lovely but duty calls." Lucy kissed her on the cheek.

"You're welcome anytime love. Stanley, see her to the door."

At the front door Lucy turned, cupped his face in her hands and kissed his open mouth with gentle lips. "I'll phone you tomorrow darling. Bye Edith."

Stanley licked the sweet pink lipstick. Disappearing over the edge of the waterfall was only the beginning. Below was rocks, boulders and rapids, all designed to splatter his brains over their seductive curves. "Bye Lucy."

Lucy flopped onto the last seat in the crowded bus, drowned and exhilarated by the lightning storm and the 'winning over' of Edith. A hot bath, a few shots of something and then Dominic's huge cock. Life was becoming as delicious as Edith's vanilla slices. The hunger years were over.

Stanley lay on his bed in the dark front parlour watching the final dregs of *The Return of the Chimpwomen*. He had seen it before but was sticking it out in the forlorn hope that someone had changed the ending. They hadn't. Chopping down all their trees was a big mistake. Death by a hundred bananas for the axe-men was probably justified but not for the squeamish.

Edith came in. "Thought you would like a nightcap love." She sat on the edge of the bed and handed him a hot mug of tea swimming with dark rum.

"Thanks mum. Isn't she great?"

"She is love but let's not rush things. You have only known her a week."

"I know, she seems too good to be true but you can't help your feelings."

"Alright love but you have plenty of time, just go slowly. I'll say goodnight now."

She kissed him on the forehead. "Night mum." He sipped the hot dark nectar and thought how lucky he was. He had survived *The Return of the Chimpwomen* and a lot, lot more.

"Please babe, I'll never ask you for anything else again."

"No Dominic I won't do it."

"Please, look, I'm begging you, just this once."

"Dominic, it's not natural. I really do think you should let someone shine a light inside your head."

"I promise I won't ask you to do it again. Just a one off so we can say we did it."

"I don't want to say I did it. Are you listening?"

"It won't hurt you. It's not like I'm asking you to jump off a roof or anything."

"Why not, It would be just as bizarre."

"Lets have a couple of drinks, loosen up a bit. I know once you get into it you'll love it, probably more than me."

She crossed her arms. "You've been watching too many weird movies."

"There you go babe, try that." He handed her a tumbler of purple shit.

"What is it?"

"Never mind, just drink it, you'll like it." She did and they drank another one. Three more followed. "Ready?"

She moved towards his painting. Her bra and panties fell to the floor. "Do you want me like this?"

"A bit closer, put your arms out each side. Yeah, that's about right."

"You're a headcase Dominic."

He closed his eyes and massaged his temples with his fingertips. "Yeah, you could be right."

Wearing only her four inch white stilettos she pressed the front of her body against the portrait of Dominic with arms outstretched and legs spread.

"Yeah babe that's nice. I like that." He strutted up behind her. "Now grind against him slow." His hands fondled her hips and slid down until his fingers probed her inner thighs. Pressing against her back he bit her neck and shoulders and eased his cock inside her. She gasped. In the unsteady light of the fluttering candles he wrapped his thrusting body around the glowing perspiration of her naked flesh, his glazed eyes aroused by the nightmare abstract power of his portrait staring back at him.

Stanley had smuggled the last fresh cream vanilla slice into his room. He knew the crumbs would burrow their way into his bed sheets but he did not care. He bit into the iced flaky layers and licked the cream squelching out from all sides as if it were Lucy's flesh. In the same millisecond Lucy screamed with orgasmic pleasure. She didn't expect that from the threesome.

The early Sunday morning daylight shone with a clear radiance. Last night's thunderstorms had washed away the suffocating blanket of heat leaving a sharp pureness in the rising garden mist.

Stanley sat, as he always did, among the scented, flowering white hordes, thinking as he always did these days, about Lucy. Listening to the joyous clarity of birdsong echoing around the long gardens made it feel like the birth of the planet. His lungs coughed back the first tobacco smoke of the day but he clung on to the moment.

He smiled when he thought about the six million concubines relentlessly multiplying in the dark privacy of their harem.

"Step right this way Stanley. That's my boy. You'll need something to carry it all in." The man with the red dyed wax moustache waved him into the bank.

"Will this do?" The rusting wheelbarrow squeaked as he pushed it to the counter.

"Fine and dandy old friend. O.K. boys, load her up. Plenty more inside."

Stanley staggered out with the overflowing wheelbarrow of free £50 notes.

"Stand back there people, give the boy some air. Same time tomorrow old friend?"

"Err…Yes…Thanks Mr…"

"Just ask for 'The moustache with the free cash.' Think you can remember that?"

He could never remember his Pin number. This was progress. "I think so."

It was all quite bonkers. But quite legally bonkers.

All his life money had squeezed his brain in a crushing side headlock. His released head now had a new headache, a replacement monster. The new stranglehold was death.

He now had a lot more to lose. Freedom, power, a new love, new dreams, a new future, a new life. Stanley, the new man.

Death would take all that away from him. Time had now become more precious than gold, more precious than anything. Like water in the desert. Without it he would die. The passing of time and life. He had wasted so much of both. Well, not any more.

With all the crap sucked out of his brain by this new enlightenment, he careered his wheelchair inside to watch a film he had been waiting twenty years for.

Edith and Cynthia spoke in quiet tones under the hot shadow of a green striped parasol, not daring to poke even a toe into the white molten heat surrounding them.

Cynthia was convinced that the mysterious spontaneous combustion of the industrial petrol mower, three gardens away, was caused by the extreme weather. What other explanation could there be. Edith agreed.

Cynthia said it had been a real blessing. The long narrow gardens now sunbathed in an enforced Sunday afternoon silence. Edith agreed.

"Did I mention Stanley's seeing Lucy again. He's quite smitten I think."

"They have only been acquainted five minutes."

Edith agreed. "That's what I said."

"She's seems more than a little risqué for me to feel comfortable. The kind one would associate with that dreadful housing estate."

"A little harsh Cynthia, she does lots of charity and voluntary work for the church."

"Oh does she now. I have heard geese fart before."

"Cynthia, you're terrible. Why would she lie?"

"I think we both know the answer to that one Edith dear."

The hushed exchanges were swallowed up by the violent heat. They sipped their boiling tea, both aware of the other's thoughts and prayed for a cool breeze. The tropical Sunday afternoon had no end.

The next day.

Stanley had to tell someone. He had already smoked ten 'roll ups' before the midday sun started it's descent. His mind was made up. This added revelation of decisive decision making was carefully filed away in the buckled folds of his dented brain.

He jabbed Lucy's number and waited. It was switched off. "Bollards." This was ridiculous, he did not even know her address. He rolled more tobacco. The summer was unrelenting. His giant plastic thermometer, hanging on the fence post in buckled submission was touching 90 degrees F.

"Tea up love. They've just said on the news, a hosepipe ban. Cynthia will go mad."

"Too late, she's already mad."

"Shush, she'll hear you and don't be so cheeky."

"Mad as a yodelling budgerigar." He shouted down the garden.

"Stanley, be quiet. What's the matter with you. Are you ailing for something?"

"My life over again." He muttered under his breath. He had other news, earth moving. He almost blurted it out but just spluttered gibberish. So much for new man.

"I think you've been out in the sun too long. Look at you, the sweat's just pouring off. I'll fetch an umbrella."

"A psychiatrist might be better."

In the enforced shade he sipped scalding black tea. Perhaps this madness thing was contagious. He rang Lucy again.

"Hello."

Her voice startled him, the mug slipped from his fingers and burning tea saturated the last three things he wanted injured. "Aagghh, hello, Lucy, It's me."

"Are you all right, you sound in pain."

"Yes I think so." He was talking through clenched teeth. "I was just wondering if you could come over tonight?"

"It's a little bit awkward. I suppose I could…For an hour… About 8 o'clock."

"Fantastic, I'll see you at eight. Bye." He checked his scalded prized possessions. Not them, please. "Any more tea mum?" It felt like a kind of madness.

CHAPTER FOURTEEN

Stanley had scrubbed up well. Sitting on his bed in the front parlour room he listened to the lightning crackling on his radio in the fading light of the approaching thunderstorm. His sunburnt shaven head, arms and clunking hands glowed a rich brown against his white shirt. In just over an hour his life could change forever.

With each dawdling minute his nervous glances at the dome shaped mantle clock increased. The old clock's arthritic hands moved with slow painful clicks until the bent small hand nudged against the seven on the cream face.

The latest M.O.T. had taken some time. *Eau De Toilette* dripped from every orifice. He blasted his head with one more irresistible whiff. One minute past seven. The radio crackled louder. Faraway thunder seeped under the open sash window.

On his lap was a small blue box. He eased open the lid. The sight of the diamond cluster ring, snug in it's velvet dark blue vault almost collapsed his heart. The light from it's reflection had a terrible beauty, like a rare orchid, that surreal goddess. The same obsessive madness that lures men to their deaths.

He closed the box. Would he die for her or kill for her? At this moment he did not know, which answered both questions. £10,000. In his other life he would have to sweat blood all year for that. Would she accept it? He clutched the boxed ring, sipped his dark rum and watched the lightning flashes creep closer.

"Where did you say you were going?"

"I didn't." Lucy blinked her eyes in the mirror. The blue eye shadow and mascara were perfect. "I know it sounds strange to you Dominic but I have more than one friend. It's called socialising."

"Don't start that shit again you cocky cow, I've got a social life and lots of friends. So, where are you going?"

"I don't have to explain every minute of my life to you or anybody. O.K. I'll be back in about an hour. See you later lover." She blew him a kiss. "Byee."

"Bitch-cow."

The gentle tap-tap Stanley had been expecting took him by surprise. Something gripped his nervous heart as he fumbled with the door. He yanked it open and her smiling face flipped him sideways. Whatever he had was terminal.

"Hello Lucy." He tried to speak and act normal. "Come on in, great to see you again. Mum will bring us some tea unless you fancy something stronger."

"No, tea's fine, I'm not really a drinker."

He glanced at his empty stained mug. "Neither am I, mum only approves of small tipples." Lucy had already guessed that. He watched her sit on the edge of the bed and stared longer than was decent at her bare crossed legs. The temptation to touch them left him twitching.

"I've missed you Stanley."

She could not have said anything else that meant so much. "Honestly?"

She leaned forward. "Honestly." Then laid her hand on top of his meaty paw. "Well Stanley, what have you got to say for yourself?"

Her pale blue eyes sucked him onto the waterfall rocks. He could still hear his smashed up body breathing.

Large droplets of rain splattered on the window. White flashes lit the room. His fingers twiddled with the boxed ring in his pocket. A sudden roaring sound of water cascaded down the window.

Edith bustled into the room. "Hello Lucy love." She ducked as a huge thunderclap almost knocked the house down. "Unplug the telly Stanley before we are all blown to kingdom come. I'll make us all a nice cup of tea to calm things down."

Lucy seemed strangely excited by it. "You're very quiet tonight Stanley."

He could not do it. His body trembled, half a ton of claggy earth filled his mouth. She would reject him. He would not see her again. Best not to push things and see what happens. "Yes, sorry." He cleared the clag from his throat. "Stumps are giving me jip tonight, must be the thunderstorm."

"You poor love. Would it help if I rubbed them?"

"Err, well, yes I think it would." He looked anxiously at the doorway. "Err, mum's serving tea in a minute."

"Oh Stanley, you do make me laugh." Her words were almost drowned out by a another thunderclap. Edith served up tea and luxury chocolate biscuits in bright coloured foil. The psychotic storm faded away with the thunder. Lucy tilted back her head and breathed in the rain soaked breeze creeping under the jammed sash window.

"That is divine." Sprawled on his bed, supported by her elbows, she eased off her black stilettos and jiggled her luminous purple toenails. "This bed is heaven."

"It's the latest mattress technology. It moulds to your body." His voice twitched.

She closed her eyes. "I could easily get used to this every night. Just heaven."

His eyes travelled down her reclining curves. "Yes it is... Heaven," he whispered.

The only light came from the orange shadows cast by the street lights. The only sounds were the plodding tick of the old mantle clock and rainwater gurgling down the guttering and drains. Distant thunder trembled across the night sky and lingered in the darkness.

"Come here." She whispered and leaned across his creaking wheelchair. With eyes half open he tasted her sweet lipstick breath. She pulled away leaving him pouting like a goldfish. "I have to go soon Stanley."

His fingers juggled with the boxed ring. "Please, not yet. I feel so happy when you're with me."

"Oh, you say the sweetest things." She leaned over and kissed him again.

"I'm not exactly Brad Pitt am I?" His watery brown eyes looked away.

"Well no but who is?"

"I am a cripple and an old cripple at that. What I'm trying to say is..." He held out the small blue box in the flat of his hand. "This is for you."

"What is it?"

"Open it. Whatever you say I'll understand."

The hinged lid softly opened. Her pale blue eyes were lit by a thousand volts from the diamond cluster ring. "Oh my

God." Her electrified fingers plucked the rare orchid from it's box. "Which finger?"

He guided it to the third long fingernail on her left hand and helped her slide it on. "Do you like it?"

She held up her hand and fanned out her fingers against the window's light. "It's beautiful Stanley, who wouldn't like it."

"So what's your answer then?"

"I'm not sure what the question is."

"I think you do."

"You're a man of few words aren't you. This looks like an engagement ring."

"Yes, it is."

"So, are you asking me to marry you?"

"If you put it like that, yes." His rigid body braced for the dagger thrust that would rip open his heart. He gripped his chariot wheels with a dead man's unblinking stare.

She looked down at the ring. "It's an almost perfect fit. How did you know?"

He shrugged, not able to talk.

"It looks expensive, was it?"

He nodded still unable to talk. Rigor mortis was setting in.

"Do you love me?"

"Yes." It was a daffy duck croak.

"Then my answer is yes, I will marry you Stanley."

He threw back his head and tears forced their way out of his screwed up eyes.

She bent over him, cupped his face in her hands and kissed his wet cheeks and eyelashes. "I love you Stanley."

"Mum." Laughing and crying now, he called out again. "Mum, I want you."

She came rushing in. "What's wrong?" A tassel shaded wall light was flicked on.

"We have something to tell you."

Edith sat on the edge of the bed with tightly clasped hands, looking at the two of them so close together. She suddenly felt very alone, almost afraid of what she knew was coming.

"Mum, you won't believe it. I've just asked Lucy to marry me and she's said yes."

Edith forced a smile but her words were genuine. "Stanley love, that's wonderful. It's bit of a shock but wonderful." She put her arms around each of them and kissed each in turn.

"Show her the ring Lucy."

"Oh yes, I like that. I won't ask what it cost. I better get us all a drink of something. Back in a jiff. You dark horse Stanley."

"You could stay overnight in my old bedroom, it's very comfortable."

For a few seconds she flustered her words. "I'd love to darling but I have to be up so early in the morning. All this is so sudden."

"Yes, of course, sorry but we can have a celebration drink before you shoot off."

"Yes, I can't think straight at the moment. Your mum's right, what a dark horse you are Stanley."

"Where the piss shit have you been, it's nearly midnight?"

"Dominic, don't shout at me, I don't like it and neither do the neighbours."

"Bollocks to the neighbours, just tell me where you've been till this hour."

"I'm not talking to you while you're in this mood."

"All right, is this better?" He lowered his voice.

"Not really."

He watched the Bacardi bottle glugging into a large tumbler. "Well?"

She spun around from the sideboard with the glass to her lips. "Feeling calmer?"

"You left your phone here, how convenient."

"A bit paranoid aren't we. I've gone for a couple of hours and you go all to pieces."

"I'm not in the mood for your clever shit smarm, just tell me where…"

She smooched over to him and stroked his long black hair. "What are you in the mood for?"

He flicked her hand away. "Just tell me what took so long."

"That's better, you're talking normal now." She stroked his hair again. "Has Tarzan boy missed his Lucy Jane? After I've told you, if you're a very good boy, I'll give you some very hot, juicy fanny and suck your big cock dry." She pulled his hand down between her legs and nibbled his ear lobe. "How does that sound?" She whispered.

He nodded. "Sounds alright."

CHAPTER FIFTEEN

Lucy dug out the boxed ring from the bottom of her handbag, flicked open the lid and gazed at the high voltage cluster of diamonds. It must have cost a packet and it belonged to her.

Juggling the two men would be more difficult now. Eventually one would have to go. A 'whopper dildo' could replace Dominic but how do you replace a multi-millionaire? She lowered herself into the fiery furnace of bathwater, sipped the midday alcoholic 'livener' and waited for the next 'problem solver' vision.

"Dear Stanley to be married to that brassy blond. Whatever is he thinking of?" Cynthia's theatrical voice had a whiff of 'over my dead body' syndrome.

Edith spread her hands. "Yes but what can I say, he seems so happy."

"My dear, happiness can be a wonderful blessing, if it lasts. I was very fortunate of course. My Harry doted on me. I mean, what do we know about her? Can she cook? The young girls these days seem incapable of anything except spawning babies."

"You don't think she's..."

"No Edith dear, that would be stretching it too far. The time factor I am referring to. I am sure Stanley is more than capable."

"Yes but you're right, everything has happened so fast. What a year."

"Unless she is carrying another man's baby."

Edith stared at her in horror. "Surely not."

"I do not think one should discount it. Society today is in steep decline. Food for thought dear."

Edith's year, before yesterday, was staggering towards madness and now…"You've really got me thinking." She watched her friend pulling a hairbrush through her long tangled mass of white hair. The brush stalled mid-stroke and she flung it down.

"My new medication's side effects are a bedevilment to me. My hair has become unmanageable. 'Lunar Whiplash,' I call it. Most irksome."

"If Stanley has to move out, I don't know what I'll do." Edith was close to tears.

"Oh no my dear, it won't come to that. If there is no baby and all else fails we could always bump her off." Her shrill laughter carried to every room in the house.

Edith forced a smile. Cynthia's grey eyes had a strange maniacal spark. This 'Lunar Whiplash' needed to be taken seriously. "I'm off to do Stanley's breakfast."

"Bye, my door is always open Edith dear." She called after her friend, brushing some moon dust off her coat-hanger shoulder blades.

The volcanic molten bath and midday 'livener' had left Lucy freefalling. She collapsed onto the sofa and pushed the diamond cluster over her 'wedding' finger. Six million was it's true worth. She would phone Stanley now and say how much she was missing him. The phone rang in her hand. She smiled, it must be him.

"Hi Lucy, it's Sue." The sledgehammer blow wobbled her brain. "Hello, Lucy, can you hear me?"

"Yes, hi Sue."

"I'm flying back next week. I wondered if you had seen Dominic?"

"Err, no...I've not."

"Does he know about my money yet from Stanley?"

"Err, no I don't think so."

"Good I'm pushing for a quickie divorce. I don't want that bastard getting half of it. If you should see him it's vital now that you don't mention it."

"I won't say anything Sue, I promise."

"Could I stay with you for a few days, I can't face going back to the house...Hello."

"It's a bit awkward at the moment...A new boyfriend."

"Ooohh, lucky you. Do I know him?"

"I wouldn't think so."

"Is it serious?"

"He thinks it is."

"I'll tell him all your past secrets when I meet him."

"Anyway Sue I've got to go."

"See you a week on Friday then."

Lucy's control of the whole situation evaporated. This could ruin her new future. She opened a new packet of cigarettes, The horizontal Bacardi bottle glugged into a coffee mug. A mid-Atlantic plane crash would solve everything.

By late afternoon the answer lay in the shallow dregs of the last swallow. Her head ached, her eyes closed on the empty mug and it slipped out of her hand. "Just remember the new plan." She murmured.

"I don't want any illegal activities under my roof Stanley."

"We shall have the marriage union stamped by the law of the land."

"Don't try and be funny, you know what I'm referring to."

"Not really. Anyway, the wedding will be in six weeks."

"You hope. If Lucy says yes. Too rushed if you ask me. Cynthia agrees."

"She would. I'm not marrying her, thank God. I'll phone Lucy to set the date."

Lucy's head snapped up with the sharp slam of the door. A sweaty faced Dominic guided his cycle into the lounge. She shuffled into the bathroom to rebuild herself.

Half an hour later with fresh coffee and a fresh cigarette it was time to sow the seeds of her recalled new plan.

"She's got two million."

"Who has?" He stopped cleaning his cycle.

"Well, it's not the old girl on the ground floor. That leaves…" She opened her mouth and raised her eyebrows in mock surprise.

"Sue?" He gaped in astonishment.

"You're soon to be ex. A gift from the lottery winners. It's true Dominic, I swear."

"The secretive bitch."

"After your divorce it could be a real pisser trying to claim half. You have to do it now. I think she's buying up property in Florida."

He paced up and down in front of her, his brain misfiring over the crunching gears. She lit another cigarette and waited. In your own time Dominic.

"You probably won't like what I'm going to say. Try to understand babe. I think it's best I moved back into my house while I sort this out. I mean, it won't look very good shacked up here with you." He bit his bottom lip and waited.

Hallelujah, Hallelujah. She was that abandoned Hollywood movie queen, Oscar nominated, sprawling on the sofa. "I'll just go along with whatever you think." Her phone rang. "Hello."

"Hello Lucy, it's me, Stanley. How are you?"

Distracted by her brief, panicked look Dominic stepped closer, trying to listen.

"Yes, fine. How are you feeling today?"

"Pretty good." Stanley laughed.

She turned her head away from Dominic's inquisitive stare, pressed the 'off' button and carried on talking. "Yes Emily, take the full course, even though you're feeling better. "O.K. Yes I will, bye Emily."

Dominic was annoyed his thoughts had been interrupted. "Yeah, so when all this money comes my way, you and me just take up where we left off. Simple but perfect, hey babe."

"Perfect Dominic."

"Yeah, being rich, I could get used to that. When's the bitch flying back?"

"A week on Friday."

"O.K. She won't know what hit her. You realise we won't be able to see each other until all this is sorted out. Too much at stake."

"Whatever you say Dominic." She almost did a back flip.

The sun touched the rooftops, stirring up the early evening traffic and filling the window with dazzling light. The excited red lycra Dominic padded barefoot around the room, talking loud into his phone to his solicitor.

Lucy escaped to the bathroom. "Hello Stanley, yes we were cut off. Tonight, to set a date. Yes, of course. Bye. Love you too." Everything was back on track. She was in control again. This would be her year.

CHAPTER SIXTEEN

There was a great deal to do and a seemingly 'mission impossible' timescale to do it in. Stanley zoomed here and there, haemorrhaging energy and achieving very little. The organisation of a wedding was far beyond his understanding but Edith had never seen him happier and now embraced the coming union with almost fanatical preparations. It might be Lucy's wedding but it would be Edith's day.

All three sat around the table with a polite difference of opinion on nearly everything from the invitations to the church or registrar's. Stanley felt quite punch drunk with it all.

"Cynthia and I are very capable of putting on a very nice reception buffet."

"Mum, why not hire a catering firm, we can afford it you know."

"I don't want shoddy food on your big day, what would people say. No, it will be a proper spread with all the trimmings, all nice and fresh."

Lucy did not want to upset Edith. "I'm sure it will be perfect."

"Thank you love, be more agreeable Stanley."

"I thought we could have the reception here." Edith continued.

"The house is too small mum."

"Not in the house love, outside in a tent."

Lucy was incredulous. "Surely you mean a marquee."

"Yes love, that's it, a 'marky' tent.

Stanley's forehead creased with pain. "In that garden. They don't make them that shape do they?"

"Yes, the garden is narrow, but we'll manage somehow."

He had visions of everyone shuffling sideways on toes bruised by collisions of crab-like movements inside this eighth wonder of the world.

"The ceremony will be in a church." He announced. He had been saved for reasons unknown by something unknown. Some bloke working in a registrar's could not claim the credit. "It's what I want."

"What Stanley wants, I want too." She laid her hand on top of his. An outrageously expensive wedding gown also had a certain appeal and a church wedding had more *gravitas*. She would have to subdue his new assertiveness though.

He was on a roll. "I thought Whitby for the honeymoon."

She pulled a face. "Whitby? You don't fancy 'The Maldives' or somewhere?"

"He hasn't got a passport, have you love?" Edith chimed in.

"All overrated in my opinion. Whitby does the best fish and chips in England and the best ale and the best speed boat trips out of the harbour."

She had no control over her macabre grin. "Whitby it is then Stanley."

He clapped his hands in triumph. "All sorted."

"I'll make us all a nice cuppa." Edith left the lovebirds cooing across the red Formica table.

"How did Dominic find out about the money?"

"I don't know. Not from me Sue, I swear. I suppose these things have a way of getting out." Lucy was thankful her sister could not see her face down the phone. "Will you be seeing him?"

"God, I hope not. We are talking through the solicitors. I'll be damned if he's getting his hands on it. There are ways. I'm staying at The Imperial Hotel for a few weeks, then I'm off again. How's Stanley, have you seen him?"

"Err, no, not recently."

"I must pop by and say hello."

"They…have gone away…on holiday…touring Scotland for a month."

"Oh, what a shame and I've lost their phone numbers. So, how's the new boyfriend?"

"Him? That's over."

"Lucy, you do get through them. Anyway, I'll see you in a few days."

"Bye Sue." Keeping all her secrets a secret was becoming tricky. She was not concerned what came out *after* the wedding because by then another key would have been cut that would open the bank vault. *Lucy's Key.* It sounded ancient and mystical.

She smiled and lit a cigarette. All she had to do was hold her nerve. She drew hard on the warm filter and her pale blue eyes followed the golden dance of *Lucy's Key*, performing a red hot Cuban rumba in the darkness. She picked up her ringing phone.

"Hello babe, remember me?"

She caught her breath. "Dominic, you sound strange. Is there something wrong?"

"Yeah, I do feel a little strange tonight. Left out, no invitation to your big day," His words paralysed her. "Nothing to say. I could talk to Stanley. We must have a lot in common except he's rich and I've still got two legs. Found your voice yet?"

"You sound pissed off."

"Yeah, that's the word, among others. So, what wedding present do you give to a super bitch-bride?"

"Dominic, I don't think…"

His loud green burp silenced her. "I know. I have given it a lot of thought so I hope you like it babe."

"If you say…"

"If I what? Say something to Stan boy. Oh, now I've told you and I wanted it to be a surprise. Do you like surprises? I do, I fucking love them."

"Don't think you can frighten me. It would be a mistake."

He burped again. "The only mistake I made was taking up with you. A bitch made in hell."

"Is that it. Are you finished?"

"Yeah, I think so, apart from your present." She held her breath. I thought Stan boy and his sweet, dear old mum would like to know you were sucking my cock in between cosy cups of tea with them. Don't you think it's the perfect gift for the perfect bitch? I do."

"Don't do this to me."

"Try and stop me. You can't, can you?" The phone went dead.

She flung the phone onto the floor. Her panicking heart left her breathless. Perched on the edge of the sofa her tightly clenched fists pushed down on her drawn up knees. Small animal sounds escaped from her closed lips. The back of her head thudded. She snatched up the phone, scanned through some numbers and jabbed one.

"Yeah, Marcus here,"

"Hi Marcus, it's me Lucy. I've got a problem that needs sorting out fast." She talked in broken gulps.

"Well Lucy Lue, fast problem solving comes at a premium rate."

"I've got the money."

"Cool, well, tell me the problem and I'll tell you the rate."

Later that night.

The four white guys in the black Audi Quattro parked three streets away from Dominic's house and at a distance from any fluorescent lighting.

They walked in pairs at a brisk pace down the deserted wet streets, past the unlit bay fronted semi's, talking in low grunts and stopped outside Dominic's house. One of them tried a key in the front door and pushed it open. The four men filed inside and closed it silently behind them.

Lucy's phone rang. She was still awake. Marcus informed her that it would be difficult for Dominic to communicate with anyone for a while with half his teeth kicked out and a steel toecap still wedged in his mouth.

She was still lying on the sofa with the curtains closed in the comforting dark and glow of her cigarette. Her sister would approve of how wisely the gift money from her had been invested. Money, the problem solver. She felt it's power, how it influenced thoughts and actions, controlled minds and inflicted pain. It was wonderful. What else could it do? What couldn't it do?

The nights alone always crawled by. The strange thing was she still missed Dominic. His cock to be more precise and the noisy exchange of their body fluids.

The violent, sudden loss of his pretty looks was self inflicted. Perhaps he would not have said anything to Stanley but why take that chance. He should not have pushed her. It's not as if he had lost his life. A good kicking was all she could afford.

Perhaps he was lucky then.

She had no more time for this. There were more important things to think about. The hairdresser and the manicurist.

In just over twelve hours she would be Mrs Kandlecake. The holder of *Lucy's Key*. She smiled. The bitch from hell would have the key to the gateway of heaven and everything beyond.

CHAPTER SEVENTEEN

Stanley was running, almost flying down the middle of Albert Street, his head tilted back in delirious laughter, his bare feet hardly touching the black tarmac. He felt the cold breath of the brittle stars in the moonless night cool his fiery legs. He had just woken from an awful nightmare. Everything was so wonderful again now.

He could see his old Ford Sierra parked at the end of the street. It was such a relief finding it again. He had searched everywhere, having forgotten where he had left it. It was a joyous sight. Edith was standing in the doorway. She looked young again. "Thought you'd like a nightcap love." He reached out. "Careful, it's hot."

His eyes tried to focus. His mum was sitting on the edge of his bed. The sweat on his face was real and so was his legless body. He closed his eyes and tried to get back to his reality dream.

"Are you all right love, you're sweating buckets."

He nodded. "Just nerves, big day tomorrow." She left him alone to drink the hot tea and rum toddy. He stared through it's hot vapours, breathing in it's sweet mixture. The nectar revived him.

Warm rainwater poured off his head and body. He was kneeling on the flooded pavement again outside Mr. Jamal's newsagents, holding the winning ticket.

If he had not stopped there. If his car had started. If he had not fallen asleep. If… Then he would not have been driving on the big roundabout at the precise split second the twelve wheeler pulled out. Winning the lottery ticket had nearly cost him his life. It had cost him his legs. Edith's humming voice entered the room again.

"If I had the choice, the money or my legs, I wonder which one I would choose?"

"You're alive Stanley, that's all that matters. You're getting married tomorrow. Be thankful for your blessings."

"Yes I would never have met Lucy would I?" Both legs for six million in the bank and finding love with a beauty like her. That seemed more than a fair exchange.

"So, what was the film like?" Edith had never seen any of his vast collection.

"What. *The Curse of the Laughing Ladyboys?*"

"Yes, what was it about?"

"You don't want to know. It's the worst film I've seen since…"

"Don't tell me…Was it *The Return of the Chimpwomen?*"

"That's the one."

"Anyway, the tent is up. A bit of a squeeze inside but we'll manage." She lowered her voice. "Have you seen Cynthia's hair?" He nodded. "Don't say anything will you."

"Just keep her out of the photos mum and away from the punch."

"Don't be horrible Stanley."

"What is she taking these days?"

"What a year. Do you think Lucy will be happy living here?"

115

Yes, I think so."

"I'm so relieved. I know it's selfish of me but I was so worried you would be moving out. That I would be alone."

"I would never leave you alone mum. I know what this house means to you, so don't worry, about anything." He held her doll's hand in his clunking paw.

"Her eyes were swimming. "What a year Stanley love, what... A... year."

Cynthia's horizontal rigid body, buried under four heavy wool blankets and a candlewick bedspread was in an advanced state of rigor mortis brought on by a Judas kiss of death. This was not the worst experience of her life but it felt like it.

Stanley's betrayal with that brassy blond bint was responsible and he needed to be punished. The putrid orange ape was placed in solitary confinement. The top drawer of the dressing table was slammed shut. A night in there would wipe the grin off his face

Only a moon outing would relieve this awful torment. All preparations had been completed. The lunar 'hair whiplash' when emerging from the dark side of the moon's 'slingshot burn' was the only side effect.

The combination of a 'muscled up' internet medication and a bottle of homemade beetroot wine had an L.S.D. trip no-one else had yet tapped into. The potential billion dollar 'high' started to melt her brain. The ten second countdown began. Right on schedule at 23.00 hours precisely, Cynthia was successfully blasted off into space on her first solo flight from 95 Albert Street.

Dark rum and heavy duty sleeping pills eventually forced Stanley's eyelids to close. What seemed like minutes later Edith tried to force them open. "The sun is shining down"

He sipped his tea with closed eyes and did not see Cynthia's stealthy approach.

Her mothball scented lips lingered on his shaven head. His bewildered surprise turned to fear when he heard "A kiss for the doomed man." The voice was Cynthia's but the kiss felt like Cyril's. He kept his eyes closed and held his breath. Mum, where are you?

"The pickled gherkins have surpassed all my expectations Edith dear."

"Did you hear that Stanley."

He pretended he was dead. The scented mothballs faded. Normality returned. He opened one eye. "Has she gone?" He whispered.

"Tell Stanley my door is always open Edith dear." She shouted from the kitchen.

Scrubbed up like a showroom urinal Stanley waited by the front parlour window for the transport to the church, devouring 'roll ups', praying his bride would turn up.

Loud beer talk gate-crashed into his room from the marquee in the sunny back garden. Laughing strangers with spider web blood lines. The nervous fidgets in his new dark blue suit increased.

Edith's smiling face popped around the door. "Car's here love."

He twisted the half smoked cigarette into the ashtray. "Well mum, here we go gathering nuts in May."

Lucy twirled around with blissful joy at the exquisite full length reflection of the rustling cream wedding gown. The sequinned silk floated on the bright morning sunlight. She held her diamond clustered finger close to the mirror. They were created for each other, this dress and this ring and she had been born to wear them. *Lucy's Key* gyrated above her glittering tiara. Her excited eyes watched the red hot rumba.

She toasted the maidenly English rose in the mirror with champagne. "Forsaking all others, for richer, till death us do part, dear Stanley." The virgin bride was ready.

The photographer did not have to ask Stanley to smile. It was stitched across his face. A jaw aching, wide, silly grin. If it was possible for vital organs to cry out with happiness, his screamed out. Never in all his life had he felt like this.

He positioned himself next to the four foot wedding cake, an 'exorbitant iced wonder' Edith called it and watched his beautiful new bride, flitting from guest to guest. He could not believe this beguiling creature belonged to him.

The heat inside the marquee curled the delicate triangular sandwiches and turned Stanley's elephant ears translucent red. They matched the different shades of lipstick planted on his gleaming head. The mug of dark rum felt good. If only all days could be so. Married life was great.

Any intentions by Cynthia to outshine the bride manifested in a dress of large gold and green intertwining leaves reaching towards a sun that paled in comparison. Her long white hair fanned out behind her in the shape of the last Vulcan bomber. The almost extinct predator hovered near it's target.

"Here she comes, don't leave me alone with her."

"Stanley, don't be silly." Lucy stood at his side and stroked his head.

Cynthia's long shadow fell across his wheelchair parked at the end of the garden. Ignoring Lucy she said "You look very handsome Stanley."

Lucy replied. "I like your dress."

Cynthia smiled at her with sharp grey eyes. "It lift's one

out of one's self dear. Which church did you say you were affiliated to?"

Lucy's sarcastic grin faded. "No specific one. It's done through the charities."

"Which charities?"

"Oh, various. I have to mingle with my guests. Stanley will keep you company."

"Don't leave …"

"What a lovely girl." Her voice hinted at manslaughter. "And a lucky one." Her shadow still hung over him.

"Better circulate myself." He tried to squeeze by her.

"I was hoping you and I could…"

"Yes, I'll be back in a minute." He roared away on his two wheeler.

CHAPTER EIGHTEEN

The Wedding Night.

Stanley hoped his new red silk pyjamas would make a big impact as he adjusted his sitting position in the honeymoon bed.

It was just past midnight and he listened to the noisy remnants of his last drunken wedding guests exchanging half hour goodbyes, emotional promises to phone before another quarter of a century slipped by. The last taxi door slammed and it sped away.

On the other side of the drawn curtains it was suddenly silent. He looked around the front parlour. It was not much of a honeymoon suite. A double bed pushed up against one wall, a small bedside table, a chest of drawers and his wheelchair left little floor space. Mercifully most of the room was in dark, flickering shadows from the scented candles scattered around the bed. Still, they had Whitby to look forward to, tomorrow.

He could hear Lucy in the upstairs bathroom. Spraying sounds, water running, soft feminine noises. She had been up there ages. What the hell was she doing in there?

Nervous warm sweat stuck to his state of the art pyjamas. Cold squirts of a bloke on a surfboard were blasted in panicking sweeping movements. Where the hell was she?

The last woman he had slept with, Denise, had no complaints but that was a couple of years ago and he had two legs then. He looked up at the ceiling. What was taking so long? He swigged a mouthful of dark rum from a small bottle then sprayed his mouth with something that had a curious fruity, anti-bacterial taste. In his hurry in the semi-darkness it could have been a multi-surface cleaner. Whatever it was numbed his mouth.

He was grateful his mum's bedroom was not directly overhead. He was anticipating a few passionate grunts at the very least. It could all be quite embarrassing.

He strained his satellite dish ears. Was that the click of the bathroom pull cord? He held his breath. Creaking footsteps descended the steep staircase with careful treads.

His head turned towards the re-hung purple door. It squeaked open on over tightened hinges. The door closed and a beautiful naked creature under white transparent lace shimmered towards his bed. Incapable of breathing with his back wedged against the headboard he watched the vision pull back the bed sheet and snuggle up to him. Was this really happening? He somehow wriggled down the bed. Her lipstick mouth caressed his neck, his face and his puckered numb lips. Slow kisses, wet and soft, crazy with a kind of love.

She seemed unimpressed with the red silk jim-jams and her fingers popped each button of his pyjama top. Tugging it free she playfully bit the flesh on his shoulders.

Kneeling in front of him she pulled the negligee over her head. He gulped. She smiled and leaned over him, teasing his mouth with her swaying breasts and pink erect nipples. The fragrance of her cool skin left him delirious. He would devour her or she him.

Her hand inched down his body and slid inside his pyjama

bottoms. His body went rigid. Her long fingers and nails teased, flirted and aroused him until the firm, joyous strokes of her hand forced repeated groans from his numb mouth.

"Is that nice darling?" she whispered. He nodded with closed eyes. She sat astride him. His long eyelashes flickered open. Her face and body glowed a rich cream in the unsteady flames of the candles. Her fingers guided him onto the downward wiggle of her rounded hips. His brown eyes became blurred with a euphoric madness.

Sitting upright, she rode him with slow urgent perfection, her breasts swinging forward with each rolling thrust of her hips.

He watched the criss-crossed shadows making love on the ceiling. Her short breaths came faster, his hands gripped her frenzied hips. His body suddenly tensed, his eyes squeezed shut against the hard gasps of pleasure that arched his back upward. Nothing else existed. It had been a long time.

She lay across him. The damp perspiration of her skin cooled his fevered body. He was floating with her moist lips on his face and numb mouth.

"Goodnight Stanley darling."

"Goodnight Lucy." Lost in the soft breathing of his naked bride against his heart and the silent, stuttering shadows of the candles he was right to think he had been saved for this one moment in time.

"Welcome home Stanley. Did you have a nice time?" Edith kissed his forehead.

"Whitby was beautiful mum."

"Where's Lucy?"

"Shopping in town."

"No need, we have plenty of food in."

"Clothes shopping mum."

"Oh, did she enjoy Whitby?"

"Err, the first day. I don't think it was her kind of place. There is something else." Concerned lines appeared on his face. "Lucy thinks the house is too small for all of us. She wants a house of her own."

"What do you want?"

"What's best for all of us really."

"She's not mentioned it before. I thought we would all be happy here. I'll talk to her when she gets back."

"I don't think you will change her mind mum."

"Edith's voice was very quiet. "Stanley, the only way I'm leaving this house is in a wooden box."

"Don't be so morbid, we'll sort something out."

"I hope so Stanley love. What a year."

Sprawling in the back of the spacious black cab was how Lucy's new life would be from now on. The rest of the seat and floor were crowded with expensive names on shiny bags. No more riding with the peasants on germ filled buses. No more poxy charity shops. No more counting the minutes for the next crap social handout. No more shitty flat life. No more threatening letters. From now on she would be somebody. A woman of some note, living in a Georgian country 'pile' with …Her phone rang.

"Aloha babe."

Her stomach swirled with unease. "Dominic, what do you want? I'm changing this number if you call me again."

"Don't do that, I would have to communicate through Stan boy. Did you hear about my bit of trouble? Yeah, I had a little accident." His voice sounded slurred, the words came slow as if he had difficulty speaking.

"No, I'm not interested. I'm busy right now, so just…"

"Don't hang up on me, I'd make you regret it. Yeah, I had two kinds of shit kicked out of me, in my own house. Can you believe it? A gang of burglars did it. Only they didn't take anything and they didn't break in. They had a key. It's a fucking mystery."

"Yes, it sounds it. I've moved on now. I think you should do the same. Alright."

"No, it's not alright. I think you were behind it and I think the police will be interested when I tell them, not to mention Stan boy and his dear mum."

"What is it you want?"

"I need money. You've got money. Simple."

"It's not mine."

"Access to it, as good as, being the devoted wife. Lets say a nice round figure, £10,000, by the end of the week. Shouldn't be a problem for a resourceful bitch like you."

"Don't be an arsehole, I'm not giving you anything. Go to your wife, she's got £2,000,000. Ask her."

"Mrs Yankee Doodle Sue has all the money tied up in property . Very complicated. Could be years before I get a penny. You owe me. Get the money or I go to the police and me and Stan boy will have a ride round the park and tell each other our secrets."

"Dominic, listen to me, I'm sure we can…"

"£10,000 cash, my house, Saturday. Then we'll be quits. Be there or I talk." The phone went dead.

She clung to the edge of the seat shaking with fear and anger. She did not think it would matter if Stanley found out after the wedding but now she was not so sure. If it came to a divorce the settlement might take years. As things were, she could have everything now. She looked at the expensive fashions in their fashionable bags, her rings, her new lifestyle, everything would be taken away.

She could not risk another beating. Dominic was on to her. She felt her teeth grinding together. Her nails ached from gripping the seat. Concealing all this from Stanley could be a big problem. She would have to get the money somehow and pay the bastard, just this once.

Dominic could ruin her life. She would not allow that to happen. If he tried to blackmail her again after this payment she swore she would have him... Killed.

"Stanley, I don't like to ask but what was Lucy crying for?" Edith whispered.

"It's her mum in the care home. You know she's got Alzheimer's. There's a problem with some payment arrears. About £10,000."

"Oh my God. What about Sue, does she know?"

"Apparently, Lucy says Sue fell out with her mum and has nothing to do with her now. So it's down to her to pay it. Anyway I'm transferring some money into a joint account and Lucy can pay it off."

"I do feel for the poor dear. Old age is a terrible thing."

The letter from Elite Care Homes for an outstanding debt of £10,000 had taken three hours to type out and print on Lucy's new laptop. She was pleased with the finished 'product' and showed it to Stanley with watery eyes. He told her she could pay it anytime from the new account which showed £100,000.

She hugged him with wet love tears, promised undying devotion and hints of a special treat later. After she had left he laid out his red silk pyjamas on the matrimonial bed with a happy whistling smile. Married life was great.

Lucy banged hard on Dominic's front door with the flat of her hand. The small holdall on her shoulder bulged with £20 notes.

It was Dominic who answered the door but it wasn't his face. It had the look of plastic surgery without instruments. The shock of the bruised, swollen mess lasted for a few long seconds. With unsteady hands she handed him the bag.

"£10,000, the bank counted it."

His ruptured face peered inside and an almost toothless broken grin was exhibited Like the evidence at a murder scene.

"This is a good start." His voice was still slurred and laboured.

"Don't try this trick again. I'm warning you."

"I suppose I should take *your* warnings seriously. You will get a bill for my new set of gnashers."

"Your brain's fuddled, that's nothing to do with me."

"It was you and you are going to pay …and…pay till I say we're quits. O.K. You owe me for giving up my life to be with you."

She stared hard at his car crash face, any sympathy lost in anger. "Dominic, you haven't given anything up. You're just in love with yourself. At least you look more like your shit portrait painting now."

"I would laugh if it didn't hurt so much. Listen to me bride-bitch, if you don't want Stan boy sharing our secret or end up in the 'nick' for this," he pointed at his face. "You'll do what I tell you to do. O.K."

Her nails dug into the palms of her hands and her blue eyes became a violent purple but her reply was soft and calm. "If we are not careful Dominic, we shall destroy each other."

He looked down at the bag stuffed with £20 notes. "That would be a shame."

She turned, her hurried footsteps crunching on the gravel drive bristling with weeds and jumped into the waiting taxi. Still seething in the back of the cab, she could not face returning to the 'bat cave' yet. "Sonia's Wine Bar" she instructed the driver.

The Dominic problem was not going away. It could ruin her life. Whatever she had to do she would do it. The fifth glass of red wine was a revelation. Persuade Sue to part with a chunk of her £2,000,000. The divorce settlement would solve his financial needs and get him off her back. She jabbed the Floida number.

"Hi Sue, it's Lucy. How are you?"

"Hi Lucy, I'm fine. Lovely to hear from you."

"I'm calling about Dominic. I'm really worried about him."

"Why, what's wrong?"

"Well, the latest is, he was burgled and beaten up in his own bedroom. His face is in a right state. I just can't believe what people are capable of."

"Oh dear, I didn't know."

"He just seems very depressed, not having a job and no money and…"

"I do sympathise but it's got nothing to do with me now, thank God."

"What I'm afraid of Sue, is that he might do something stupid. I don't want that on my conscience, do you?"

"Of course not but I cannot be held responsible for anything he does."

"I know but now we are both aware of it, I could never forgive myself if something did happen. Could you?"

"Well, no Lucy but I almost had a nervous breakdown living with him, so why should I care what happens to him?"

"Because you're a caring person Sue. That's why you became a nurse."

"So what would you do?"

"Sort out the silly divorce settlement so you can get on with your life with a clear conscience."

The line went quiet and was broken by a long sigh. "The money is all tied up Lucy, it's out of my hands now."

Lucy raised her voice. "You must find a way. He needs that money, you must give it to him, it can't be that difficult."

"I've already told you. The solicitors are handling everything now. I'll only be advised by them."

Lucy's eyes raged. "I don't believe you. You could pay him if you really wanted to." Her fist came down on the table. "You heartless bitch, always thinking of yourself, you selfish prat. Piss off then."

"Lucy." Sue's shocked voice was cut off.

Half the people in the bar saw the phone slam down. Red wine splattered like blood. Ignoring the stares, she swayed to her feet and made the perilous journey to the door, bumping into tables, swearing at onlookers. The sharp Autumn air revived her spinning head. 'The Dominic situation' was out of control. It was a 'puke up' feeling.

She hoped she would not have to do what she was thinking.

CHAPTER NINETEEN

Stanley felt miserable. The beautiful bride he married only two short months ago was now tinted with mildew.

Wrapped up against the chill of the late Autumn winds his eyes followed the white flying clouds blowing across the brilliant blue sky. He was sitting next to the four foot wedding cake again staring at his new bride in her stunning cream gown, chatting and laughing with brown and red leaves swirling around her like confetti.

His eyes filled with tears. He was so proud of her. Was his imagination playing other tricks? Suggesting she was another person, a stranger, someone he did not know. It was bewildering.

"What are you doing out here love? You'll be blown away." Edith called out.

"Just thinking mum."

"The man on the telly said this is the tail end of Hurricane Delilah."

Delilah, he remembered, ensnared Sampson with her beauty then robbed him of his great strength by cutting off all his hair. Burnt out his eyes and enslaved him. Not the sort of girl to take home to meet mummy. He shivered. It was just a very ancient story. Women like that did not exist any more.

"Lucy's back from shopping Stanley." His mum shouted.

She greeted him with a peck on his cheek. "Darling, you'll catch your death sitting out in this gale."

You wouldn't want that to happen would you, he thought. She smelt of alcohol more and more these days. She seemed in a happy mood but she always was after her 'fashion fix' and midday tipple.

"You've got some colour in your cheeks." She pinched his face.

"It's the wind." he replied.

"He's always had that." Edith laughed. "I'll make us all a nice cuppa."

They all went inside. Lucy sensed his sombre mood and planted a sloppy kiss on his shaven head. She held his hand across the table, seducing him with her smile and blue eyes. It was imperative she kept him sweet and happy. She told him awful jokes. He sniggered. She told him more. He laughed. She stroked his face with her fingertips and bit his elephant ears. He cooed. She whispered rude promises. He panted.

What had he been worrying about? He expected too much, lived alone too long. His imagination was out of control. He vowed to make greater allowances in the future and become a 21st century man. Caring, sympathetic, touchy, feeling. Tactile bollocks.

"Cooee, anybody home?" Any hairs he had left on his head shot up.

"Come on in Cynthia, you must have heard the kettle." Edith greeted her.

She plonked herself next to Stanley. "Good afternoon everyone." Her long, scraggy legs became entangled with the shiny bags rammed under the red Formica table. Her head ducked down. "Ooohh, someone's had a busy day."

"I like to look nice for Stanley." Lucy stroked his head.

Cynthia's eyes blinked a few times. "Of course you do dear. Tell me, how is your charitable works progressing?"

It was Lucy's turn to blink. "It's finding the time. It's been so hectic these past months."

"What a shame but it does give you the opportunity to pursue other things." She cocked her head under the table again.

"If you want any advice on fashions don't be afraid to ask." Lucy's icy smile was met by Cynthia's icy grey eyes. At least Stanley's mind was at peace again.

The opening of a new cocktail bar in the High Street was a very early Christmas present for Lucy. She had always wanted to sip champagne cocktails on a high swivel, chrome and leather stool under soft blue lights.

The thousand pounds she was spending every week seemed an outrageous amount in the beginning. Now it was barely enough. Seduced by every new fashionable garment, shoes, handbags, jewellery, cosmetics, hair stylists, beauty therapists, taxis everywhere and a hefty drink tab. It all came to a pretty penny.

She was now dipping her toe well into four figures. The plastic cards glowed white hot. Looking good came at a price she would tell Stanley.

The unimaginable had now become normal. But normal would never be enough. A £1,000,000 Georgian 'pile' had caught her eye. A chainsaw approach would be needed for the hacking through of the umbilical cord and abandonment of the mother-in-law in her bat-cave. A red Mercedes convertible sprawling on the gravel drive in front of the 18th century three storey mansion completed the dreamy orgasm.

Keeping Stanley happy was crucial but easy. He seemed very grateful for all her performances on the super mattress. It was usually all over before she could count to ten. Her phone rang.

"Alhoa babe."

A sickly sliding feeling rose from her tummy. "Yes Dominic, what do you want?"

"What do you think bride bitch? I've got a new set of gnashers, cost the moon and stars but I think you'll be impressed. The dental guy wants his money."

Her angry breathing prevented her speaking at first. "I'm not paying you any more. I told you last…"

"£10,000 by Friday or it's the police and Stan boy. I've got nothing to lose. Have you?" The phone went dead.

She now realised this parasite would devour her from the inside. The last thing she wanted was the police and Stanley rummaging around in her complicated past life. Her fall would be quite spectacular. She would have to pay him again but £10,000 payments were unsustainable. She needed a different way out.

When she arrived home Stanley's face was red with excitement. "Great news Lucy. The builders are starting on Monday morning."

"Starting what?"

"The extension, our new bedroom suite and summer room. We could be in by Christmas. Isn't it just fantastic. Now we won't have to move."

She was horrified. "You are joking."

"No all the plans are passed. I knew you would be pleased." He zoomed off to tell Edith with the builder's contact letter on his lap.

Lucy closed the door on the excited chatter and laughter from the kitchen. The pen in her hand snapped in half, smudging her fingers with blue ink. This was not her day. She reached into her bag for the small bottle.

"This film is absolute garbage. What's it called?" Lucy whinged.

"*The Thing from the Black Country.*" Stanley was snuggled up to her in bed.

"Is that why it can't communicate with anyone?"

"Shush, you'll miss the best bit."

In the last ten minutes of shrieking mayhem, *The Thing* was zapped with 5,000,000 volts by an ex-traffic light cleaner. For him it was personal.

Stanley rubbed his hands together. "I have seen worse, much worse"

Lucy shook her head and slid down the sheets. "What would Stanley like now?"

He kissed her nose. "I love you so much. I wish I could have met you when I was younger."

"But then you would have been arrested." She smiled and tapped his forehead.

His face had the confused expression of a stunned duck. "It's a crazy life. You're so precious to me."

"Am I darling. Ooohh, what's this?"

The marathon sex that followed was a personal best for Stanley. Minutes rather than seconds. He wallowed in the afterglow. Life did not get any better than this. Rum, movies, sex with a goddess, someone to hold in the night. Wonderful. He was snoring within minutes.

It wasn't that keeping Lucy awake. It was Dominic. The silent hours of darkness allowed her imagination to run free. Some time after 3 o'clock with the last details of a new plan churning around inside her head she fell asleep.

Late on Friday morning Lucy climbed out of a taxi at a mini shopping parade and walked the short distance to Dominic's house with £10,000 cash rammed in her shoulder bag. Cold rain sleeted down. Her face was hidden under a large umbrella. She hurried over the weed infested gravel drive and knocked on the door.

The door opened. Dominic's smile looked expensive. "Like them?"

She pouted. "Yes I do." All the swelling on his face was gone, so was the bruising except for the dark rings under his eyes but that was probably due to his lifestyle. His long black hair was swept back behind his ears. "Well, are you going to ask me in?"

He hesitated and bit his bottom lip. She always had ways of surprising him. He glanced up and down the road with suspicious eyes. "Yeah, come on through." He stepped back and felt her expensive perfume waft over him. She still moved in a delicious way.

"It's nice and warm in here. Can I dry my coat?"

His mind was on the contents of the shoulder bag but his eyes were all over the tight lines of her dark blue 'designer' skirt and top. "Yeah. You seem very relaxed about all this. I expected a hard time."

"What's the point in fighting about it. It's not my money anyway."

He nodded, still biting his bottom lip. The thick bundles of £20 notes now being stacked in neat piles on the coffee table had his full attention. "Any drink in the house?" she asked without looking up.

Another surprise, he thought. What next? He poured the Bacardi close to the money and they clinked their dark tumblers over the stacked piles of £20 notes. They both emptied their glasses and he topped both up again.

"So, how's married life?"

"It's all right."

"Just *all right?*"

"We get along. I do miss some things."

"Like what?"

She nursed the tumbler close to the upturned corner of her mouth and her hips swayed in tiny movements. "What do you think?"

"I think I'll have another refill." This was the last thing he expected. What was the bitch up to now?

She moved around the table. "Let me pour it." Standing close to him she filled both tumblers almost to the brim. Her fragrance clawed at his resistance. "Shall we drink to old friendships." They clinked glasses, her body brushing against him. They drank without speaking, almost touching, hardly breathing. The glasses were drained.

She placed her hand at the back of his neck and gently pulled his face towards hers. Her kiss was gentle, intoxicating. She kissed him again, deeper, urgent, her tongue probing, her body pushing hard against his, her fingers ripping off shirt buttons. Breathless, frantic they fell onto the sofa. She yanked down his trousers and he watched her greedy mouth devour him with luscious, frustrated noises. He groaned as her blond head bobbed up and down with joyful motions. Deep, hard, slow, bliss.

She stood over him and slipped out of the top and skirt. She unclipped her red bra and let it drop to the floor. Then, legs apart, she bent over the arm of the sofa.

"Is this how you want me?"

He positioned himself behind her. "Yeah, this is how I love it." He placed his hands on her hips and eased down her flimsy red panties. "Beautiful" he murmured.

She closed her eyes, felt his fingers fondle her and gasped…"Oh my God." This is what her body had ached for in all those recurring dreams. Dominic rode her from behind with an urgent, almost violent desire. A non-stop motion of slapping thrusts against her bottom, his fingers digging into her hips until he collapsed, groaning on top of her.

They lay on the sofa, arms and legs intwined, as if they had never been apart. As if the previous few months had never happened.

"You see how it could be Dominic, you could have everything."

"Yeah, perhaps you marrying him could be the best thing that ever happened."

"I think so, for us, I mean."

"Yeah, £6,000,000, that's a big wedge." He stared at the piles of £20 notes on the coffee table with the fevered eyes of a gold prospector.

She rolled underneath him. "Anything you want baby. Please fuck me again."

He kneeled in front of her and raised her ankles onto his shoulders. She closed her eyes and experienced again the forgotten pleasures of his dynamic love making.

It was late afternoon when Lucy left and walked the short distance back to the mini-shopping parade for a taxi. Dominic was too busy thumbing through the piles of 'twenties' to notice she had not called for one from his house.

Her change of heart was surprising but probably inevitable when he thought about it. She had married for money and was now unhappy. She wanted him back. Had found out she could not live without him, could not resist him. Understandable.

CHAPTER TWENTY

The last twenty minutes of *Confessions of a Serial Artex Man* was a bloodbath. Stanley and Lucy watched mesmerised as the entire village hunted over five counties for the escaped *Mr. Twirly Whirly*. They cornered him in a barn still performing his vile deeds. He pleaded insanity but the crazed villagers ripped him limb from limb.

"Night night Lucy. Builders start tomorrow. Sleep tight."

The clanking chains of a skip being unloaded outside the window at 8 o'clock in the morning dragged Stanley from the horrible dream of *Mr. Twirly Whirly*.

Lucy watched the half dozen builders from behind the net curtains, each uglier than the last, all hungover from the weekend. So, these were the men who were about to change her life with a poxy extension.

Stanley zoomed around outside, plans unfurled, organising tea, cracking jokes, taking photographs. This was a big day. She watched the chaos gain momentum. She had her own plans. It would be easier to split the atom than separate Edith and Stanley from 'the bat cave' of 97 Albert Street but she was alive again. Although Dominic's mercurial cock had to take some of the credit, it was something else. Invisible, highly addictive and irresistible. *Lucy's Key.*

Late Autumn turned to early Winter. Dark nights descended. The shorter days were cold and wet. Christmas baubles were on sale before Halloween.

The extension was rising steadily towards the roof. Tea, coffee, milk and sugar was costing more than the bricks and cement. Stanley had assumed the position of chief engineer on the project. Everybody was happy.

"Time left, 2 minutes to place your bets ladies and gentlemen." The young, fast talking compere on the live T.V. roulette game smiled into the camera. Dominic bit his bottom lip and tapped the arm of the sofa. He was down to his last £1000. How could he have lost £6000 since yesterday? The bastard thing was rigged. He would win it back, just a matter of time. What to do? Safe, small bets or play with style?

"Time left, 1 minute to place your bets." said the compere with the permanent smile. Dominic jabbed at his computer. 15. Black. £1000. The bet was acknowledged.

"Table closed. Good luck everybody." The compere half turned towards the spinning wheel. The mad rolling dash of the white ball clung to the outside edge of the black ring, racing against the wheel, spinning in the opposite direction.

Dominic watched spellbound as it slowed and edged towards the red and black numbers. The white ball hovered over the rotating numbers, fell into a box which spat it out and hovered again. He held his breath and gripped his kneecaps with his hands.

The ball bobbled into a black cubicle. He closed his eyes and prayed. The blurred numbers slowed. He opened his eyes.

The compere announced the result. "34. Black. Even. High Result." Dominic stared at the screen in disbelief. His last thousand pounds was gone in the time it takes to boil an egg. The sickness in his head moved down to his stomach. He knocked back a tumbler of neat Bacardi to dull the pain and picked up his phone.

Lucy was sitting on her favourite chrome and leather swivel high stool, sipping her third champagne cocktail when she received the call needing extra funding. "Won't be a problem will it babe?"

"No, Dominic, it won't be a problem." Her reply was calm and measured.

"£5000 will sort me out babe. Tomorrow evening, yeah. Love ya."

"They're up to the guttering." Stanley proudly announced. Lucy felt a couple of back flips coming on. "I don't know what to say."

"I know, I feel the same. At this rate we'll definitely be in by Christmas."

"I can't wait."

"We'll deck it out like Santa's grotto."

"Ooohh, how exciting." She needed another drink. Stanley studied the plans with renewed enthusiasm.

"Sooner or later I'll hit the big one. I'm that close. I can smell it babe." Dominic had not shaved for days. His clothes were creased. His eyes had a wild, deranged stare. His unwashed dark hair hung around his dark stubble in greasy strands. His hands shook when he counted the money. He was a mess. His new addiction had the same power as any drug and was just as destructive. Lucy watched him carefully. It could work in her favour.

The white ball danced on the black spinning wheel.

Dominic watched with bloodshot eyes. Nothing else existed. He leapt off the sofa, arms aloft. "Yeah, yeah," he screamed. "Did you see that. What have I been telling you. A winner." He was close to cracking the code now, very close. A pattern was emerging. He jotted down more calculations. A few more spins, a few more risks. "I'm so close babe."

She kissed his cheek. "I have to go. I'll speak to you later in the week."

"Yeah, yeah, night babe." His eyes were on the gold dust screen.

"The soil pipe is being connected to the main drains today." Stanley was ecstatic.

"Why don't you take a photograph?" Lucy's reply had an embalmed feel about it.

"Good idea, I'll get the 'before' and 'after' shots. Do you want to watch them?"

"I'll experience it through your photos."

He looked disappointed. "I just thought…Where are going?"

She kissed his forehead. "Try not to fall into the trench again."

"Who told you about that?"

The taxi was beeping. She blew him another kiss and was gone.

Lucy restricted her visits to Dominic's to one a week, phone calls the same. She would see him today. Wrapped against the cold and prying eyes she rapped on his door. It swung open on it's new bolts and lock. Dominic was even more dishevelled. He had lost weight and had still not shaved. The lounge curtains were permanently drawn. The only light came from the spinning roulette wheel on the screen.

"I can't get any more money for a while Dominic. This account's almost empty."

He switched on a lamp. His face looked strained and gaunt in it's light. "So just transfer some from another account. What's the problem?" His eyes became annoyed slits in his fatigued face.

"The problem is I have to be careful. Stanley's not stupid. If he finds out all this money has gone from the account he'll stop everything."

He shuffled across the room with round shouldered frustration and threw himself into an armchair. "A few poxy grand, it's a pittance to him. He's too bollocked up to enjoy it anyway. Someone ought to put him out of his misery."

Lucy helped herself to a drink. "That would suit me. I would get the whole six million." He never heard her forced laugh but the words *six million* had a sublime effect on his aching head.

Neither said another word, perhaps afraid of what they were thinking, perhaps waiting for the other one to suggest the unthinkable. The roulette wheel spun again and his body leaned towards it, hunched forward on the edge of his armchair. The happy compere announced the winning number and Dominic seemed to slump. He poured another drink and tapped the armchair in sullen silence.

"I can get you some more money baby but I am restricted on the amounts I can take out and the times. You do believe me don't you? All I want now is for us to be happy again and not argue." She hugged him and kissed his neck.

"Yeah but I did believe you once before, remember."

"I know and I'm so sorry about that. This is why I'm making it up to you now. Just think Dominic, we could have it all if Stanley was not here."

He gripped her arms. "What do you mean?"

She stood up. "If anything should happen to him. He is accident prone. Think about it. Right now I need some cock."

"They've done a cracking job on the manholes. We're all connected up to the main sewers now." Stanley's face was beaming. "Wait till you see the photographs"

"Can't wait, I have to go over to…"

He shuffled through a thick wad of prints. "This one is Mick cutting into the main sewer pipe. Look at the size of his angle grinder."

"Mmmhh, fascinating."

"Now, this one is really impressive…"

Every time Lucy saw Dominic he looked worse. His dark whiskers had become a stubbly beard. His hair hung in greasy strands around his pronounced cheekbones. His dark eyes seemed to glitter in the smallest light and his arms and hands were in a permanent state of agitation. The clothes he once filled out now appeared to hang on him. He was a mess. The Greek god was in meltdown.

"Everything's driving me nuts." he ranted, prowling around the room. "Where's the money you promised?"

"I have some here baby but he's frozen the account. I can only get small amounts at a time. £500. That's it for … Well, I don't know, to be honest."

"Shit. The tight-arse bastard. You're his wife, put your foot down, threaten him, do anything you have to."

"What, *anything?*"

"Yes anything. Push his wheelchair under a bus. I'm not bothered."

"But that's murder Dominic."

CHAPTER
TWENTY ONE

At the end of November cold sleety rain fell in squally showers all day and night. Stanley was in a joyous mood. "The builders reckon they will be finished by the middle of December. The stair-lift goes in last. Won't it be wonderful to have our own proper bedroom and bathroom."

"Yes darling, just wonderful."

"What film are you watching tonight love?" Edith came in with a pot of tea.

"*They came from Outer…*"

"Don't tell me. I've seen that one. *They came from Outer Space.*"

"No, *They came from The Outer Hebrides.*" A bit of a cult horror classic now."

"Ooohh, it sounds good. Are you watching it Lucy?"

"I can't wait."

"You'll end up a film buff just like Stanley. He's got hundreds you know."

Lucy's smile resembled a fart.

On December 1st a hard frost left everything white until midday. Dominic's state of body and mind had not improved.

"Is that twat of a husband of yours still being a prick?"

"He's even stopped my weekly allowance now baby. There's nothing we can do."

"That's what you think." He gulped down some pills with a tumbler of rocket fuel.

"I'm just as frustrated as you are Dominic. I'd love to know how much interest £6,000,000 earns in a day."

He bit his bottom lip and stared at her. His eyes turned black. "You know what you said the other day, about having it all if he had an accident."

"Yes but I was only joking."

"Were you? Could have fooled me. I don't think you would grieve too long if dear old Stan fell out of his wheelchair."

"That's a horrible thing to say, I'm very fond of him."

"We'd be doing him a favour, rotting away in that contraption every day."

"This is my husband you're talking about."

"Save your tears for his funeral."

"You want him dead?"

He seemed to shrink away from her. "I'm just saying £6,000,000 is a lot of dosh. It's wasted on him. What if he outlives you, then you'll never get your hands on it. Stranger things have happened."

"So you want him dead?"

"Do you?"

She lit a cigarette and turned her head away from his dark gaze. "Yes." She could have been confirming the order for a catalogue dress. It was a game of dare where no-one backs down and it spins out of control. They sat in silence with the curtains drawn watching the white ball racing around the black and silver roulette wheel.

"What would you like for Christmas?" Stanley was propped up in bed with Lucy.

"Oh, just you tied up in a red bow."

He laughed. "I'll surprise you. I've got my eye on something really special."

She kissed his shaven head. "How sweet darling. Would you like me to surprise you?"

"Great, there's nothing I would like more."

They settled down for *Cannibal Corgis from Hell*. "It's based on a true story," he explained. "It's one of my favourites."

"You're expecting me to do it?" Dominic was more than agitated.

"Well I can't. The spouse is the number one suspect. The papers would have a birthday. New younger bride, legless millionaire, all his will made over to me."

"Yeah. *You,* not me. Why should I trust you again?"

She stroked his greasy hair. "Because I love baby. I always have. You know that's true. This was meant to be, can't you see that. With £6,000,000 we can do anything, go anywhere, be whoever we want to be."

"Are you sure you get the whole spondulicks? What about his mum.?"

"I witnessed the will being drawn up. She gets the bat-cave and half a million which would be the 'interest' by the time everything's sorted, give or take. £6,000,000 for a few minutes work, that's the bottom line."

He bit his bottom lip and looked around at the shambles of his life. "If I did agree, *if,* just how the hell am I supposed do it?"

She breathed out. "It will be easy. Every night he watches a film, sometimes two, in bed or in his wheelchair. I'll make sure he's in his wheelchair and 'sparko.' Drink and his prescription drugs will do that. He'll have his back to the door. His skull was fractured in the car accident. Any hard blow to his head can be fatal."

"A hard blow with what?"

"A poker I will leave under the backroom window where you come in. I'll leave the catch off, just ease it up. Take the jewellery and money from the top drawer of the chest of drawers. Scatter half over the floor with the poker to make it look like a botched burglary and take the rest with you. Leave by the same window."

"What about his mum?"

"She'll be at bingo between 8 o'clock and 10.30. We do it at 9.o'clock."

"How do I get away?"

"Same way you got here, on your cycle. Come down the entry, the back gate will be unlocked. Leave it just inside so no-one can see it. I'll lock the gate when you've gone, so they think you've climbed over."

"Where are you when all this is happening?"

"Upstairs having a bath. I come down and confront you."

"What?"

"Dominic, listen to me. We have to make this look real. You will have to beat me up and do a really good job on me."

He stared at her. "Have you gone completely cuckoo."

"Don't you see, it will make the whole thing totally believeable."

"It's a lot to take in, let me think about it."

"We don't have the time Dominic, we have to act soon."

"All right but it's a big decision, we are talking murder."

She looked hard at him. "I thought you had guts. Do you want to stay as you are?"

"I didn't say I wouldn't do it. It all feels too rushed."

"There is nothing to connect you to him. Burn all your clothes after. Dump the jewellery down the local tip in the 'non-recyclable' skip and we're home free."

"What about D.N.A.?"

"You're not leaving any bodily fluids behind, are you or fingerprints or anything. You have no criminal record, no motive. You're off the police radar. You'll be in and out the house in two minutes and gone. Just think Dominic, £6,000,000. This chance will never come your way again."

His eyes seemed to turn black. "Alright I'll do it."

She placed her arms around his neck and kissed him gently on the mouth and cheeks. "It must be done before the end of the week."

"But it's Wednesday now."

"I know." She kissed him again. "I'll phone you tomorrow."

Stanley was cock-a-hoop. "The builders will definitely be finished next week Lucy. We can choose curtains and carpets now."

"Alright darling, I can't wait."

"I've never felt such happiness. It's all down to you."

"Thank you darling. I love you too." Her fingers stroked the lines of his face.

Lucy spoke calmly into the phone. "It has to be tomorrow, Friday, 9 o'clock because he'll be upstairs in the new bedroom sometime next week and that just complicates things. I'll go over it again with you now and then the next time we see each other will be in the house at 9 o'clock. Now listen carefully…"

CHAPTER
TWENTY TWO

On Friday morning it tried to snow. Stanley sang and whistled for most of the day hoping it might coax more snowflakes out of the sky but he never saw any. Lucy had left the selection of the carpets and curtains to him. He hoped she would like his choices. They would be fitted next week when the builders had finished. An hour or so was spent riding up and down on the new stair lift. Fantastic. By 3 o'clock the light was fading and by 4 o'clock it was dark. Oh glorious Winter he thought.

Outside the mercury in his giant plastic thermometer dropped below 32F. He turned up the thermostat. A short list of films were selected for later on. Lucy would like these. She was still out shopping, perhaps buying his Christmas present.

He laid out his brand new pyjamas on the bed. Shiny lime green, guaranteed to impress the lady in your life, it said on the packaging. He agreed. The silky smooth material felt good against his skin. They did not make him irresistible but the almost fluorescent purchase made a *dash*. Two dozen fat 'roll ups' were spread, twisted, licked, smoothed and crammed into his large 'Cigi tin'

Edith fluttered in with freshly mashed tea. "Ooohh,

there're new," blinking at his pyjamas. He grinned back. "Unusual colour love but they're very nice." He grinned again and sipped his tea between yawns. He was bored and hoped something exciting might happen tonight.

Lucy's stilettoes clattered down the side entry. Funny, he thought, she always used the front door. He posed with his arms outstretched. It stopped her in the doorway.

"Shit, you gave me a turn."

He laughed. "Sorry, I didn't mean to startle you. What do you think?"

She composed herself, cursing the fluorescent lime green pose that had scratched her jangled nerves. She leaned over him, a mixture of cold air, stale perfume, stale alcohol and cigarette smoke. "Yes, they're lovely." She glanced at her watch. 6.15. "What film are you watching tonight darling."

7.30 p.m.

"I'm off to bingo now love. I'll be back about half past ten. I've got my key for the back door." She kissed him on the cheek. "Have a nice evening both of you."

"We will Edith and you." Lucy waited until she heard her padding down the entry and then walked into the kitchen. She crushed four of his painkillers in an eggcup of hot water, poured it into his stained mug, filled it with dark rum and stirred it.

"Here you are darling, a nightcap with your film." She stroked his shaven head. He smiled and puckered his lips. She hesitated for a moment then cupped his face in her hands and kissed his mouth just like a lingering farewell. "Goodnight darling."

His brown eyes misted. "I know what a lucky bloke I am. I've been blessed." She nodded with a smile and left the room.

8.15 p.m.

Dominic paced around his house. His brain and body were jumping. What had he got himself into? He could still pull out, this was barking. The shakes pursued him from room to room. He gulped down a tumbler of rocket fuel with some pills and felt it seep into his maddness. The truth was he was more afraid of what Lucy would think of him if he did not do it. What would he say to her? How could he face her again?

The lure of £6,000,000 was not normal. He felt it's seductive power warping his brain, dragging him to another place. He had no control over that.

He ran his hand over his black resprayed cycle. 19 minutes exactly from his front door to 97 Albert Street. Another 5 minutes to get inside. He would have to leave at 8.35. Latest. He looked at his watch. 8.30. Shit. He tucked his long dark hair under his hat and pulled it down over his ears. He flexed his fingers in the brown leather gloves while he jogged up and down.

He took a deep breath. He was ready. Just do it.

8.35. p.m.

Leaving only his bedroom light on, he locked the front door with a double click and sprinted off on his cycle, hardly aware of the cold sleeting rain or anything else. A black figure on a black flying machine, swallowed up by the black night.

Lucy rose from the white steam of the hot bath. Her body glistened in the flickering light of a horde of candles. Dominic should be on his way.

8.45. p.m.

Despite the screaming horror in the corner of the room Stanley's eyes kept closing. The dark rum 'nightcap' had switched off his brain. Warm and light-headed he floated away with his movie. A half hour doze never hurt anyone.

Lucy winced at each creaking step of the staircase. She crept across the dark back room to the window, pushed back the swivel catch and eased the sash window up six inches with gloved hands. Lifting the heavy brass poker from it's ornamental stand, she placed it below the window. Was he awake?

She tip-toed over to the parlour door and put her ear against it. Snoring, lovely dreaming snoring is what she heard. She sat back in the dark outline of a chair and watched the sleety rain trickling down the window. Her luminous wristwatch flashed 8.56. The only sounds in the darkness were running rainwater and faint snoring.

9.02. Where the hell was he? The black shape in the window startled her. It disappeared. Seconds later it was back. Barely breathing, she watched the sash window edge up. It shuddered and stopped. The black shape swore and squeezed through the narrow gap.

She rose from the chair, whispering "Dominic, under the window, the poker."

Her voice made him jump. His groped around and found it. "Is he in there?" he whispered back.

"Yes, asleep, be quick."

His careful footsteps made no sound. Listening at the door he gripped the poker tight in his right hand. He turned the round door handle with tiny movements and edged the door open.

There he was, just as she said, in his wheelchair. The top of his shaven head tilted back, looking as fragile as an eggshell. From behind he heard a whisper. "Do it."

He crept up behind him and raised the poker over his head. In the corner of the room the naked young virgin spreadeagled on the sacrificial bed screamed in terror.

The poker swung down in a medieval style execution. It thudded into Stanley's skull. His whole body jerked forward as if electrocuted and crumpled onto the floor. Dominic stood over him, breathing heavily, watching the blood seep from his ears nose and mouth. The indentation across the top of his head was now bleeding.

There was no movement, no sound of breathing, no sign of life. He had killed him. The sense of relief was overwhelming. He felt almost elated. It had been easier than he thought it would be. The sacrificial beauty was still screaming. He started to back out of the room when he heard the whisper behind him.

"The jewellery, top drawer."

He jerked open the wood drawer and grabbed all the expensive gold and diamond sparklers and wads of cash, ramming them into his pocket, dropping some on the floor with the poker. He backed out the room again, half turning in the doorway, he bumped into Lucy.

"Slap me, do it" she ordered him. He hesitated then hit her across the face. It felt stangely satisfying. He hauled her to her feet by her bathrobe. "Again," she said. This time there was no hesitation. The hard slap with the back of his hand sent her reeling onto the floor again. He rubbed his hand. It felt good.

He stood over her like the dark shadows had stood over him in his own bedroom, using his head as a football. "I know it was you bitch. Admit it." She shook her head and dug her nails into his balls. He screamed and knocked away her arm. His clenched fist swung down and cracked against the side of her head. She sprawled on the carpet, stunned, groaning with pain.

He kneeled next to her. "Hurts, doesn't it." He dragged her to her feet again, holding her up by the lapels of her towel robe. Her head was limp and bloody. The pathetic simpering moans coming from her split lips seemed to excite him. "How does it feel bitch." He slapped her face again, hard as he could. Blood spurted from her nose. He was beginning to enjoy it. As her head rolled back he let go. She fell onto her knees and her body slumped forward.

Panting with pleasure, his stinging hands wet with blood, he hauled her up again by her bathrobe. "Had enough babe? Think that will fool them?"

Her mouth, full of blood, gurgled "This will." From her deep robe pocket the hidden fish knife arced up in a vicious thrust. All of the serrated 6 inch steel blade was rammed into his body. They clung to each other, their faces only inches apart. Two lovers staring into each other's eyes in a brief final dance.

The waltzing couple staggered against the red Formica table and sank slowly to the floor. Lucy's hand still gripping the bone handle of the knife jammed in his ribcage. Both his hands were still clawing feebly at hers.

The entwined lovers lay gasping for air under the table. The serrated steel tip of the knife had ripped open his lung Blood poured through the torn opening and his lung began to fill up.

"Help me." His dark eyes were glazed with death. The rising blood at the back of his throat tried to strangle him.

She kissed his bloody mouth with her bloody mouth. "Sorry baby." He stared into her eyes knowing he was dying and not understanding why.

The premeditated murder of Dominic was the only part of the plan she had not told him about.

Edith's night could not have been better. Two winning cards and a boozy laugh with the girls. She put her key in the back door and stopped. Why was the window half open? Everything was in darkness. Usually lights were left on. She opened the back door and flicked on the kitchen light. A groan came from the unlit back room. She popped her head through, flicking on the light.

"Oh my God." Her eyes widened in disbelief. She covered her mouth with her hand. Lucy was lying on the floor, her face a bloody mess, her blood splattered bath robe ripped from her shoulders. Lying next to her was a man halfway under the table with a knife sticking out of his body. She looked at the open parlour door.

"Stanley, Stanley." she shrieked, rushing across the room. She stopped in the doorway, paralysed with horror. Her son was crumpled on the floor in front of his wheelchair with trickles of dried blood on his mannequin white face from his ear, nose and mouth. His twisted body was lifeless.

She almost fainted and fell down beside him, cradling his head in her arms, rocking back and forth. "Oh God, no. Please, no."

CHAPTER
TWENTY THREE

Nobody in Albert Street had ever seen anything like it. Sirens, dozens of flickering blue lights, ambulances, police cars, paramedics, fluorescent coats moving in and out of number 97. Crowds of people gathered under umbrellas around the blue and white cordoned off tape. Rumours flashed up and down the chaotic street.

"What happened?"

"There's been a break-in."

"Someone's been murdered."

"Stanley and a burgular are dead."

"His missus has been taken to hospital."

"What about Edith?"

"She's been carted away as well."

"Oh my God."

The low murmur of continuous gossip fed upon the mayhem.

Dominic had done a good job on Lucy's face. Every inhaled breath through her broken nose made her wince. She only had blurred vision in her inflamed right eye, the other was swollen shut. Both lips were split and puffy. Both sides of her face were bloated with purple bruising. With two dead men in the house this was her alibi.

Lying in the hospital bed Lucy wanted to smile. The plan had worked. The £6,000,000 was all hers. Less than six months ago she was on Social Welfare. Now she was a multi-millionaire. Her, Lucy Marmalade. She couldn't believe it. Sharing it with Dominic was never an option. No witnesses to anything. No-one to implicate her with anything. A botched burglary. A heroine fights for survival. It was perfect.

She was suddenly exhausted. Her mind wandered to the extravagant heat of The French Riviera. What an impact she would make there among the rich and the famous and the beautiful. This wealthy English Rose.

"How are you feeling this morning?" The doctor sat by the side of Lucy's bed.

Her reply was weak. "Groggy… and frightened."

"The sedative we gave you for traumatised shock will make you sleepy. It was a terrible thing you experienced but you have nothing to be frightened of now. Unfortunately we do have some bad news to tell you."

"Yes, I know what you are going to say. He's dead."

"The paramedics could do nothing. He was pronounced dead at the scene."

She closed her eyes. A tear squeezed onto her cheek. "We've not been married that long. God, it's all so unreal."

The doctor and nurse looked at each other with puzzled frowns. "We are not discussing your husband. We are talking about the intruder."

Lucy opened her eyes. "My husband is…"

"Stanley is in intensive care with a fractured skull. I'm sorry, I thought you had been told."

She stared in disbelief. "He's alive?"

"We don't know the full extent of his injuries yet, there could be brain damage or other complications but he is being closely monitored."

She closed her eyes again with a strangled sob. Her fingernails ripped into the bed sheets. Perhaps he would die from his injuries. She could only hope.

Stanley's new nightmare world was a moving black wall of vomiting pain floating in the darkness. Invisible waves, stalking him, crawling inside his skull and crushing his brain with it's gut wrenching power. He cried out but made no sound. In his despair he prayed for death to release him from the horror inside his head.

The two detectives who interviewed Lucy were young, sharp and smelt a rat.

"Hope you are feeling better now Lucy."

"A little. Thank you."

"We just need to know what happened in your own words on the night Dominic Joggle died."

"Yes of course but I have given a statement."

He nodded. "Just a few questions as well. Your relationship with Dominic, how would you describe it?"

"Well, Dominic had his problems. Halfway through a divorce to my sister. Alcohol issues. A big gambling problem. Debt problems. He talked to me about them from time to time. I suppose I was a good listener. I liked him and still don't know what possessed him to destroy our lives." She shook her head and wiped her eyes with a ball of tissue.

"Did he ever visit you in your old flat on Station Road?"

"Err…Yes, a few times."

"More than five?"

"It could have been, it's hard to remember an exact number."

"Did he ever stay overnight?"

"No, why should he? Look, I thought you wanted to know what happened."

"Just building an overall picture. The jewellery we found on him, which you have identified and the large amount of cash, did you ever mention it to him?"

"Yes I think I did tell him how generous Stanley had been. Stupid really but I never dreamed he would…Anyway…The cash was for the builders."

"The catch on the sash window where he gained entry had not been forced. Edith told us it was definitely locked the day before on Thursday."

Her face twitched. "Yes that was me. The window had been sticking. I asked one of the builder's to fix it. I must have left the catch off. God, I feel awful about that."

"The knife. You said you grabbed it from the dining table. How did it get there?"

"I don't know. It was just lying there."

"In Edith's statement she cleared the table before leaving for bingo at 7.30."

Her body stiffened and she stared at the clever twat. "Now I remember. It had fallen at the back of the table. I saw it when I put my shopping away which I always leave under the table. Yes, it was after Edith had gone out. I just placed it back on top."

"Did you recognise him in the struggle?"

"No, it was too dark. He grabbed me before I could put a light on after my bath."

"I see." He thumbed through a pile of papers and pulled

some out. "Going back to your contacts with him. The phone records show you had long and frequent conversations with him. Before his wife walked out, up to the day before he died." The two pairs of eyes watched her and waited.

Lucy did not flinch. "Yes I've already told you, the guy had a lot of problems. I talked them through with him. I wish to God I hadn't now." You're shooting in the dark. Clever twat. "Am I being investigated?"

"When anyone is killed in violent circumstances we have to be thorough in our reports Lucy. Just a few more questions and then you can go." She watched the smarmy arsehole study fresh pieces of paper. "Your bank statements show recent cash withdrawals of £10,000 on two occasions and other large cash withdrawals over a short period of time. Can you tell us what the money was for?"

"No I can't, that's my business, how I spend my money. What right have you got to go snooping in my affairs?"

The one called 'clever twat' leaned back in his chair and clicked his biro annoyingly fast. "All right Lucy. Thanks for your time, we understand the trauma you've been through. You can go home now. We may need to speak with you again."

They waited for the door to close. "What do you think?"

"She's too calm. Not once did she show any regret for killing him. No remorse or feeling for anything. No mention of her husband's condition. The only time she got upset was about the money. She came across all wrong."

"Yes, she did. Too detached. Too arrogant and cool with her answers, as if they had been rehearsed Back to the drawing board."

Edith, Lucy and Cynthia sat around the red Formica table, their strained faces jaundiced by the yellow glow of a table lamp.

"I still can't believe it. What has he done to bring all this suffering down on him?" Edith's voice was shaking.

"All life is a mystery my dear." Cynthia.s hand dwarfed Edith's in it's reassuring strokes. "I shall keep a night vigil while you are in this vulnerable condition and pray for Stanley's life."

"Thank you Cynthia. Yes we shall all pray tonight. How are you now Lucy?"

"I don't think I shall ever recover." She touched the bruising on her face.

"You were very brave dear," Cynthia replied. "Admirably so, faced with that madman. Thank God you were playing bingo that night, Edith dear. One dare not contemplate the consequences if you had not."

"I blame myself for not fastening the window." Lucy covered her discoloured purple face with trembling hands.

"No, no, you must not do this to yourself. You have been through enough." Edith wrapped both arms around her fearless daughter-in-law and held her close.

"I'm just thankful we have each's support to try and get over this awful nightmare." Lucy's muffled, sobbing voice were answered with solemn nods.

The cold December rain slanted down and pawed at the locked window.

Lucy rocked back and forth in Stanley's wheelchair like a demented caged bear. Her loose fitting bath robe was rumpled and odorous. Her pale blue eyes, dulled by heavy cigarette smoke and warm alcohol stared at an unknown terror.

Her neglected hair, now a dingy yellow, was greased back with thick gel. Her left eyelid hung like a shop window canopy over her once closed eye. The black bruising under her eyes was darker, as were the purple welts each side of her face. A greenish tinge lay under her skin. Her broken nose continually ached and the muscles in her face hurt with every deep drag of her cigarette and swallow of neat alcohol.

Those two swarmey arsed coppers could never come close to what she had done. They were a joke, a pair of pissing bum boys, like Dominic, like all men. All he had to do was smash Stanley's skull while he was sleeping. What could be simpler than that? But he managed somehow, to fuck it up. She thumped the arms of the wheelchair with her clenched fists. The plan had not changed. The call of The French Riviera was still as strong. He may not recover. She clung on to that.

The tantrum passed and she went looking for a new bottle. She looked into the round distorted glass of the convex mirror. A hideous monster smiled back.

CHAPTER
TWENTY FOUR

The black wall of pain pressing down on Stanley's head sometimes receded into the grey mist of a stiff cardboard fog, it's agonising grip relaxed as if it were taking a rest. In these brief moments he could breathe again. Then it would return, angrier than ever, intent on punishing him for taking advantage while it was away. A slow, gleeful crucifixion of his brain. He prayed so hard for death, many times.

The release came with the heavenly exultations of an angelic choir. The black wall began to melt and it's vile contents oozed into a strange glass bottle. The miracle was performed to a chorus of *Hallelujah, Hallelujah* and an explosion of pure white light.

"He's back. Oh my God, he's back." Someone was crying. It sounded like a woman's tears. Other excited voices joined in. He dare not open his eyes, he would be blinded but it all seemed so real. In the next ward a choir belted out another Christmas carol. The voices around him were gentle and caring. They drove away his tormentor. Imprisoned it in a shape shifting glass bottle. He was afraid the bottle might crack and it would escape. Don't leave me alone with it. Please.

A soothing voice reassured him. "It's all right Stanley love, you're safe, you're back with us now. God bless." It was safe to rest for a while. He did feel tired.

The observation of the Winter Solstice and Stanley's homecoming to 97 Albert Street were celebrated on the same day.

Edith's happy tearful face and festive red jumpsuit greeted him at the front door. "Welcome home love." She hugged his shrunken body and kissed his hollow cheeks.

"You need feeding up." She was choking with emotion.

His pale features creased with a weak smile. The lines on his face were deeper and longer. "Where's Lucy?"

"In the bathroom. Wait till you see the decorations love." She wheeled him through the parlour. The room where he had been nearly bludgeoned to death was exactly the same. It was as if nothing had ever happened in there. He wondered if he would be able to sleep in that room again. Work on the extension had been stopped. The new bedroom was not finished. He sat next to the Formica table and started rolling a cigarette with unsteady hands. The baubles on the pre-Thatcherite Christmas tree were new, as were the red flashing lights. The astronaut's 'G' forces that had squeezed his brain returned. He turned his head away from them before he started retching.

He had felt worse. He was after all, back from the dead.

He could not help thinking the lottery ticket was a curse after everything that had happened since he won it. Footsteps on the stairs quickened his heart. But if he had not won it he would never have met Lucy. His love, his saviour.

The staircase door opened. "Hello darling." Her face was puffy and strained with black circles under her eyes but she still looked beautiful to him. She held his head against her body. "I'm so glad you're home Stanley."

Unable to speak, he curled his arms around her waist. It would be all right now. He just needed time to sleep and recover. "I still can't believe it, Sue's husband" he whispered.

She pulled away. "I don't really want to talk about it Stanley."

He looked flustered. "Yes I'm sorry. We've all been through enough. What a bloody nightmare." He shook his head. "It's hard to think straight. Sorry."

Edith finished laying the table. "Let's try and put it all behind us and just enjoy Christmas. Just be thankful we have each other. We'll start by putting some meat back on your bones Stanley love."

He nodded. "We're still in the front parlour then."

"Yes love, your new bedroom won't be finished until the new year now."

Struggling to concentrate, he closed his eyes. His words became slurred. "I'm feeling a bit tired today." His head nodded and seconds later a gentle snoring filled the room.

"He's so weak Lucy, we must keep a careful eye on him."

Lucy stroked his face. "Don't worry, I'll be with him all the time from now on."

When Stanley woke the next morning he could see snowflakes through the small gap in the curtains. Drawing them back he watched the thick mass of large flakes swirling up and down the street. The grey cold light showed everything buried under a thick white quilt. It seemed to energise his slow brain and slower movements. The first snowfall of the Winter always had that uplifting effect on him.

After the confines of the hospital, being home again felt

wonderful, despite his drowsiness and a sledgehammer banging against his skull. He yawned and stretched.

"Morning love, sleep all right?" Edith scurried in with a mug of hot strong tea, laced with evaporated milk and three sugars.

"It's nice to wake up in your own bed." His words were sluggish. "Where's Lucy?"

"Out shopping would be my guess. That girl certainly loves her clothes."

He seemed embarrassed. "Well, it is Christmas."

"How are you feeling today?"

"Not too bad, apart from a belting headache."

"The doctors said you would. Take your tablets and I'll get you some breakfast."

He sat by the window watching the deranged snowflakes. She could have been here, when he woke up, on his first day out of hospital. He could not understand why she wasn't, if she loved him as much as she says. His mood darkened. Mum was still doing all the cooking. It dawned on him that Lucy had never cooked a meal.

Snap out of it. What was he thinking? After all she had been through. He was a selfish prat. He felt ashamed. She had probably saved his life and his mum's. Her lovely face bashed in by that lunatic. Too long the bachelor, cocooned in his own little blinkered world. His headache was worse.

He would make it up to her. He started thumbing through a jewellery catalogue. He was so looking forward to this Christmas. It would be one to remember.

Lucy was sitting in one of those establishments that could not make it's mind up what it was. A pub, a coffee house, a snack bar, a restaurant…The place was a pain in the arse but nowhere else was serving alcohol yet. The third large red wine had just dissolved the last cobweb spun across her brain from the delightful bat cave. She was a desperate woman in need of a desperate plan.

The panoramic street level window she was sitting in was full of shoppers and snow.

Opposite her was a bald, middle aged twat, twiddling with an untouched pint of beer, three newspapers, a slice of pork pie and another morning to kill. He irritated her just by being there. Annoying tossers like him should be banned and only allowed in libraries and garden centres.

If she was going to do this thing. Get rid of Stanley. It would have to be done soon, while he was still weak. But how? Any weapon leaves a wound. Any drug or poison can be detected. Although she had heard of an almost undetectable poison in anti-freeze. Something to think about. Might take a long time though. Some kind of accident? Possibly. One more bang on the head would surely finish him off.

The harmless tosser opposite leaned towards her. "That's the best stuff to drink." He pointed at the glass she was holding. "For heart attacks. Red wine."

She raised her top lip in a sneering smile. Piss off you old twat.

"Says in today's paper, the biggest killer in Britain." He suddenly had her attention.

"Oh yes, happened to a mate of mine last year. Went to bed. Never woke up. We're all at risk. Smoking for instance, clogs all the arteries up. I know…"

She let him waffle on. A heart attack. Death by natural causes. It was perfect. Stanley was high risk. Legs amputated, cracked skull, puffing on them 'roll ups' all day, vegetating in his chair. No-one would be surprised. The heart just stops. A tragic death. No-one would question it. No suspicion would fall on her. Yes, it had to be done now while he was still gaga. But how to induce it?

The old twat was still waffling on. Smiling Christmas shoppers hurried by, chatting excitedly in the deluge of falling snow.

The red wine slithered around her brain. Killing someone was not the shitty experience she thought it might be. The truth was she found it pleasurable. That night she held Dominic's life in her hands. To see the light dimming in his eyes. To feel and hear his last breath in this world. Nothing else had ever come close to that feeling. It was an explosion of a thousand orgasms.

Her eyes refocused. Laughing small children quick-stepped by. Santa was on his way. Bless their little hearts. The harmless tosser had not come up for air. She stopped him mid-sentence with a sharp "Goodbye." His open mouth followed her out.

Lucy listened to Stanley's snoring with loathing and frustration. It was 3 o'clock in the afternoon, the day before Christmas Eve. The parlour room was in the half light of a short Winter's day. The lack of sleep from last night's pneumatic snoring had also left her irritable. He was sitting in his wheelchair, head slumped forward to one side. He slept a lot during the day she noticed. The snoring continued it's plodding march. She felt no court would convict her on grounds of compassion if she done him in now. A pillow over his face would silence him.

She almost cried out at the eureka moment. A pillow would silence him forever. 'Bingo,' as Edith would say or whatever crap they shout out now. A pillow. He suffocates, he stops breathing. Heart attack, suffocation, what's the difference? He's dead. Died in his sleep, just like the old twat said.

She sprawled on the bed and watched him for an hour. For short intervals he would lapse into silence, not breathing. Then with a sudden intake of breath and a rapid putter of his lips, he continued his melodic shanty. It occurred to her that if pressure was applied at the critical moment of breath holding, he would never recover. Goodnight Stanley.

Why not do it now? No, Edith was in the next room and she wanted him in a weakened state when her eleven stones of body weight pushes down on his face with a fluffed up pillow.

Her whole world was now focused on tomorrow, Christmas Eve. The emergency services would be stretched and probably in chaos which would be in her favour. By keeping him awake all day and somehow drugging him at night it should be fairly easy to suffocate him. After all, she had got away with one murder. On the night of peace and goodwill to all men she would kill her husband.

Stanley made a waking noise and came out of his slumber. "Hello darling," she greeted him with a kiss on his forehead. "You've been snoring your head off."

"Hope I didn't disturb you." His head was thick with pain.

"No, don't be silly darling but I want you alive and alert tomorrow on our first Christmas together."

It made him smile. Yes, he would make a special effort on that very special day.

CHAPTER
TWENTY FIVE

Stanley was chasing his legs over a wild landscape of red shifting sand. He no longer recognised the long skinny legs he used to walk on. They were now deformed mutations. White broken bones jutted out at strange angles. Putrid flesh had grown over the projecting jagged bones that wobbled under it's stretched, transparent canopy.

They hobbled along, just out of reach, in awkward jerking movements like a pair of broken pistons, shadowed by a frenzied cloud of rabid, fluorescent green flies whose domed red eyes reflected the delirious stench of rotting flesh.

Breathing hard in the alien atmosphere, his aching arms felt like stone. The wheelchair tilted to one side into the soft sand which threatened to suck him under. Exhausted, he watched his legs stop, turn and tap one foot impatiently. Game over.

"Remember when you could do this Stanley?" The voice came from the leg mutation. It performed a well rehearsed tap dancing routine and finished with a demented, mad Irish jig, kicking sand all over his tormented watcher in his half buried chariot. It was a mocking reminder of another life Stanley's damaged mind had almost forgotten.

"Don't you wish you could do that"? The voice said.

"Yes, it would be wonderful."

"Well you can't. You never will. You're dancing days are over freak head."

"Bastard." Tears filled his eyes.

"Stop feeling sorry for yourself." The lopsided legs ambled away. "Look at me."

The red landscape around him was being submerged by water. It rose quickly, devouring everything. It freed his trapped wheelchair and he floated in a new world. He watched his legs splashing around, showing off, balancing upright, doing the back stroke. They dived down and surfaced close to him. A hefty kick sent the wheelchair into a fast spin like a fairground waltzer.

"It's great fun here Stanley." The persecution continued with more kicks at the spinning wheelchair. He felt dizzy and sick. He retched over the side. His eyeballs left their sockets. His head was exploding. "Stop for God's sake."

He heard calm, soothing voices coming across the water. A sharp needle broke the skin on his arm. Sweat cooled his face. The spinning slowed down and the legs swam away. He gently bobbed up and down in his drifting wheelchair on a flat ocean of water as darkness closed in all around him.

She kept beckoning to him. He opened his eyes. She floated towards him. The goddess of the seas, naked with no face, laid her hands upon his head. Perhaps she could take away his raging headache.

"Stanley, you need to be baptised. You want to be saved don't you?"

Yes he nodded, he wanted to be saved.

"Don't be afraid, it only takes a few minutes." She lifted

him out of his wheelchair and laid him in the water. It felt cold and unfriendly.

"Am I going to die?" He could not see her smile, he only felt the strong hands pushing his head under the water's surface. Further and further his head was forced down under the powerful thrust of her arms. He began to panic, his hands could not release her grip. He could not breathe, she was drowning him. His body thrashed about as if in the death grip of a crocodile.

Through the last rising air bubbles his horrified eyes could see the watery face of Lucy smiling down at him.

He lashed out at the dark shape holding him in it's suffocating possession.

The mug of hot tea crashed to the floor. "Stanley, it's all right, you were dreaming."

He gulped in air, staring at Lucy's startled face. "You silly boy, shouting out like that, it was just a bad dream. Now look what you have done." She bent down and picked up the empty mug, minus it's handle, off the sodden carpet.

Stinging sweat trickled into his unseeing brown eyes that still held the terror of his ordeal. She sat down on the bed. "Are you all right darling"? Still gasping for air, he cowered away from her. No, he wasn't alright. She had just tried to kill him. He continued staring, it was still hard to breathe. "You have been poorly again darling. I'll fetch some more tea." He watched her leave the room.

He was still shaking. What the hell was that all about? His head was a fuzzy, thumping mess. Dreams are one thing, this was insanity. As if she would do him any harm. The doctors had warned him he might have nightmare flashbacks, but this? Perhaps he was going insane. He did not feel right in the head. 'Poker aftershock' he called it. He looked into the mirror hanging over the mantle. His face was porcelain white. He searched for teeth marks in his neck, convinced a vampire had swooped in and sucked him dry with a ghastly nocturnal feast.

Lucy came back in with fresh tea, an assortment of pills and his tin of 'roll ups.'

"Here we are darling, it's Christmas Eve at last." She kissed his forehead.

Desperate for a smoke and still feeling 'off his rocker,' he nodded without making eye contact. The sweet nicotine was dragged into every shrieking nerve end. He didn't feel very *Christmasy.*. He coughed up the last mouthful of water from his lungs and felt better. Just like one of his films, the dream played out before his unblinking eyes. *The Mysterious Case of Stanley Kandlecake* they would call it. A great 'whodunnit' for the festive season.

"Just popping out darling, shan't be long." Lucy called from the doorway.

He readjusted his eyes, feeling ashamed and guilty over his dream. "Bye Lucy." His cracked voice managed and swallowed more nicotine with his pills. It's Christmas Eve. Snap out of it and get in the mood you miserable sod, his nodding head told him. The next fattest 'roll up' was selected from his tin and lit. A Christmas to remember. That's what he wanted, more than anything.

Lucy sat in the large picture window of the establishment that served everything, sipping another red wine, watching the rush of Christmas shoppers stream by. Her fingers removed the wrapping from 'The Strongest Tape in the World.' It was black and heavy, specially engineered for the job she had to do. A £10 investment for £6,000,000. Not a bad return. Tonight was *the* night.

He would be asleep before 9 o'clock. His medication and dark rum would guarantee that. Unconcious was how she wanted him. The black tape was an insurance policy. She would bind his wrists to his stubs. Thick paper tissues would prevent any hair or skin being ripped off when she removed them. She would then sit on his body and suffocate him a pillow. She ordered another drink.

He plonked himself down in his usual seat opposite her. The old smiling twat with his three newspapers, overflowing pint and *two* slices of pork pie. "Merry Christmas."

She wanted to slap his face, at the very least. "Merry Christmas." Her sneering reply and continued gaze out of the window did not faze him. He babbled on about the commercialisation of everything. She turned further away and hoped he might choke on his pork pie. Save her the task of ramming it down his throat.

Edith had told her she was spendin the night in Cynthia's house. Probably till the late hours, which was perfect. She would not raise the alarm until Christmas morning Get everything right. What if the silly old sod, Edith, came in tonight? She would just have to go hysterical earlier. It wouldn't matter that much, either way. It was vital she kept him awake. He was sleeping a lot in the day. She wanted him exhausted.

She drained her glass and stood up. The old twat was still droning on. Picking up her handbag she swung it over the table, knocking the full pint glass of beer into his lap. He jumped up with saturated trousers. The pork pies went flying. "Bloody hell."

"Sorry about that. Merry Christmas." Open mouthed, he watched her flounce off.

Stanley was feeling a little better. He watched the odd flakes of snow floating on the frozen air from the parlour window. The house was tropically warm. He felt sorry for anyone having to work in these freezing temperatures. He used to hate it. A familiar carol drifted through with Edith's singalong and nostalgic cooking smells that he sniffed up with relish. The presents were wrapped and laid under the tree. Films to look forward to and of course his new wife to hold throughout this special night.

It all helped to push aside the awful memory of that dream. How could he have such thoughts? Where did they come from? His shame and guilt left him digging his Lion's paws into his stubs. He promised himself he would make it up to her.

His eyes were hot and heavy. The light was already fading in the room by the early afternoon and his head began to nod in the warm silence of the house.

"Stanley, don't go to sleep darling, it's Christmas Eve." Lucy's voice pleaded.

His eyes jerked open. Shit, he had bollocked up again. "Sorry, it's these tablets, they knock me out." He shook his head which only made him feel dizzier. The cold air she brought in helped revive him. He tasted her alcohol breath as she spoke. "I know what would be nice. Hand delivered Christmas cards to all our neighbours instead of just posting them through the door. Then we'll have a lovely visit to the park. Go to our little bench by the trees. What do you think?"

"Sounds great." She continually surprised him. How wonderful she was.

It was dark when they returned to the house. Stanley was glowing with nips of rum and festive wishes from his neighbours. Everyone could see what a happy couple they were. Stanley was a lucky man. The park trip was cold and magical.

"You're going to be a movie star." She held up the latest camera. "Our first Christmas together, captured forever on film." Another surprise. He rubbed his hands together. Why didn't he think of that?

Edith greeted them, blowing her nose. "Don't come too close, I've got this awful cold. You don't want this over the holiday."

"Can you take some film of me and Stanley. Just press this button Edith." Lucy cavorted around him in silly poses, laughing and joking. Whoever watched it would see the happiest couple in the world. The high spirits of comparative newlyweds, a blessed union of love. The devoted wife and her cock-a-hoop hubby. Lucy had the beautiful memory she wanted. The night crawled on.

7.30 p.m.

Edith shuffled into the parlour with her face in another tissue. "I'm feeling lousey Stanley. I'm just going for a little lie down. Cynthia might pop round later. She has her own key to the back door. She won't disturb you."

"Alright mum, take some paracetamol." Edith padded up the stairs.

"What a shame but do we need Cynthia interrupting our night? We don't want to frighten her, do we?" She laughed.

He leered back. "Well, no, but she is a comfort to mum. She won't stay long."

She glanced at the mantle clock and cursed the 'long streak of piss' "We do need some privacy darling. Who knows what we'll be doing."

8.00 p.m.

"Cooee, anybody home?" Cynthia's voice echoed through the house.

"Edith's having a rest. She's feeling a bit run down with a cold." Lucy called through the parlour door.

"Oh the poor dear. These's bugs can be so tiresome. I shall see if she wants anything. The trials and tribulations of life one has to endure." She clunked up the stairs enquiring if her friend was awake.

The opening scene of *Septic Tank Drivers from Hell* was a shocker. Stanley was transfixed. "I'll make us a drink." Lucy said and left him to it. She stood at the bottom of the stairs listening to Cynthia prattle on. Plenty of time yet. She poured out a generous measure of Schnapps and woofed it back. The clear liquid burned the yellow fur off her tongue. She had another and felt her brain tilt. It put her in the mood for… She smiled… Anything.

She pulled out the roll of black tape from her shopping holdall and felt the weight of it's lethal power in the palm of her hand. She turned to Cynthia's footsteps coming down the stairs and tucked it back inside the holdall.

"I fear Edith has influenza, poor love. She needs a careful eye on her. I shall return later to ensure her condition has not deteriorated. One cannot be too careful."

"I was about to put the bolts on for the night. We both still feel very nervous."

"Very understandable my dear. In that case I shall stay a while longer. I know it must be a slight inconvenience to you but I have to know she is all right. She is running a high temperature."

"I can look after her." Lucy's cold stare had a knife thrust feel.

Cynthia's coat hanger shoulder blades twitched inside her cardigan. "I am afraid I must insist on staying a little longer my dear. We are very old friends you see. You can be assured

I will not disturb you. It will put my mind at ease. I'm sure you understand."

Lucy's nails dug into her palms. Her face hardened. This batty old twat could ruin everything. Another voice told her there must be no arguments, no suspicious behaviour, everything must be normal. She tried to smile and her strained voice finally spoke with a calmness that surprised her. "Yes, of course Cynthia. What time were you thinking of going?"

"Depending upon her condition, shall we say 11 o'clock. I will just say hello to Stanley." She knocked on the parlour door and walked in. "Good evening Stanley. You are looking very festive my dear." He fidgeted in his red silk 'honeymoon' pyjamas, trying to concentrate on the bloody carnage on the screen while throwing nervous glances at Cynthia's looming frame. "I shall sit with Edith for a while longer tonight and then return tomorrow morning."

"Thanks, err…Cynthia."

"I shall be bringing my mistletoe with me on Christmas Day." Her long hair trailed out of the room with her shrill laugh. He must get a large bolt fitted on that door. She left an odour of beetroot wine and mothballs that lay across the room like a weapon of mass destruction. He listened to her size 12 shoes negotiating the steep staircase and returned to the carnage on the screen.

Lucy cursed the barmy twat again and her mother-in -law for being ill tonight of all nights. She concentrated on his favourite 'hot toddy.' Half a mug of tea, topped up with rum and the added zing of Schnapps stirred in.

"Here you are darling, a nightcap tipple with your film."

"Thanks. Although I'm not supposed to drink alcohol with all these tablets."

"It's only a spoonful, that won't hurt you. Come on it's Christmas. Cheers."

He smiled. "Cheers." He swallowed a mouthful. "That's got a kick."

"It's good for you darling, get you nice and relaxed for later." She stroked his shaven head and kissed his lips. Then lifted the drink to his mouth. "That's it darling." He drank with his eyes half on the screen and half on his beautiful wife, each mouthful tasting better and swallowed quicker than the last. The slaughter of the rural country folk by the jovial septic tank driver, nicknamed 'Psycho Sid' by the press, had caused nationwide panic. It was the best film he had ever seen.

"I'll get you another." She listened at the bottom of the stairs. No sound. Had the barmy old twat fallen asleep? She had to find out. She crept up the stairs and peered around the bedroom door. Edith was invisible under a thick duvet, her hand lost in Cynthia's prizefighter's mitt who was sitting by her side in an armchair with her head tilted back in open mouthed heavy breathing. She tip-toed down the stairs. The hour was getting closer. Excitement rippled through her. She binged on the waves of taboo pleasure whose orgasmic power left her breathless.

She handed him the lethal fresh drink. "I'll be wearing my "Mrs Santa Suit' later on. It's called 'A naughty festive wish.'

His brown eyes glistened with alcohol and lust. "Can't wait to see that."

"Good boys always get their wishes come true."

The erotic vision pummelled his senses. "When are you…"

"Patience darling. It will be worth waiting for." She stood in the doorway. A carnal dream, eager to please him. "I'll be coming down the chimney at midnight."

CHAPTER
TWENTY SIX

10.30 p.m.

Lucy stood at the bottom the stairs listening to Cynthia's snoring. Barmy bitch. She poured a large quantity of brandy into a fresh glass, turned out the light and sipped it in the darkness. The divine moment had come. That supreme feeling of exploding energy and power over everything, when anything was possible.

She licked the inside of the empty brandy glass and silently crossed the room to the parlour door. She watched Stanley's head sliding down the headboard, swimming with alcohol, strong medication, exhaustion and poker aftershock. The pneumatic drill snoring started at once. She returned to the bottom of the stairs. As if in recognition, the answering call from a fellow snorer drifted down the stairs. It seemed the whole house was asleep.

She grabbed the hefty roll of black tape, scissors and thick paper tissues and walked barefoot into the parlour room. She stood over his vibrating red silk body. Working with calm, deliberate movements, as if she were spinning her silk web around a trapped, buzzing fly, both of his arms were jammed against his side and the paper tissues laid around his wrists and stubs. The black tape was unfurled with a sharp ripping noise and wrapped in tight jerking motions around the right wrist and stub.

He continued to snore. With half the tape used up she leaned over him and trussed up the left arm and stub with manic glee. The room had a tropical heat. Sweat dripped off her nose, leaving dark splodges on his red silk pyjama top. Stanley was now prepared for slaughter.

On the other side of the drawn curtains a group of young girls exchanged loud squealing talk and laughter as they tottered by on ridiculous high heels. She froze as they passed by the window, angry with the interruption.

She looked down at her husband's sleeping face and lifted up the pillow with both hands. "Goodnight darling Stanley." She covered his face with it and pressed down with unnatural strength.

Strange muffled groans from another world filtered through the pillow. Sitting astride him she felt his back arch up and his body heaved against hers with the same urgency as their frantic lovemaking. His trapped arms strained and buckled against 'the strongest tape in the world' Her distorted face managed a twisted smile. Try all you like. Won't do you any good darling. She pressed her knees into his shoulders and felt them rise and fall like a wrestler trying to beat the count of three. Her arm sockets almost dislocated with the strenuous downward push.

She lay across his face. Bearing down with fresh determined force she felt him grow weaker, felt the life being squeezed from his lungs with each loud tick of the ancient mantle clock and strained grunt from her parted lips.

There was no movement now, no feeling of life under her triumphant murderous breathing. She had done it. He was dead. She sat upright on his chest, her shaking arms still holding the pillow over his face. She laughed with ecstatic relief. Short, almost sobbing bursts of pleasure and delight.

"Hello, it's only me."

Lucy turned her head towards Cynthia's open mouthed, shocked face.

Like excavated stone monoliths from a lost civilisation they stared at each other in silent disbelief, not moving or breathing.

A shrieking werewolf leapt out of the television. Lucy jumped off the bed, screaming with hatred. Cynthia screamed back in terror, flinging herself through the door, slamming it shut after her. Long strides on wobbly legs carried her to the back door. She fumbled with the key as Lucy's bare feet clomped across the floor behind her.

The key turned, she wrenched open the door and dashed outside, throwing herself at the walled gate, fingernails scratching against the bolt. Lucy appeared in the doorway clutching a knife. Cynthia's fingers clawed at the frozen bolt. Lucy closed in. With a muted fearful cry she turned and loped off down the dark garden, almost colliding with a scaffold pole on the unfinished extension.

She could hear Lucy's bare footsteps very close behind her and glanced back as she stumbled forward, banging against a scaffold pole. Blood spurted from her nose. She staggered on over the frozen debris of broken bricks and concrete.

"Cynthia, you're being silly. It's not how it looks. I won't hurt you." She tripped over a discarded plank. "Shit, bastard builders." Come here you barmy old bat.

Cynthia tried to hide in the darkness of the garden, her desperate breaths of frozen clouds hanging in the night air. She was going to be murdered. Now, in her best friend's garden on

Christmas Eve. She slipped, could not get up and crawled over the minefield on grazed bloody knees and bloodied hands.

"Let me help you." Lucy's voice was reassuring and calm. She knew the old twat had fallen over somewhere in front of her. Cynthia tried to stand but her legs buckled under her. She sprawled among the broken bricks in the blackness at the bottom of the garden. Gulping back her hysterics, her body and voice paralysed with terror, she watched mesmerised as Lucy's dark shape grew larger.

She stopped, six paces away. "I can see you. What are you doing down there?" The dull gleam of steel waved from side to side. "All this silliness. We'll laugh about it tomorrow. Let's go back inside where it's warm." Cynthia held her breath and waited, her hand trying to prise a broken brick out of the frozen ground.

Lucy leapt forward, the knife raised above her head. Her bare feet landed on black tarpaulin covering the newly dug fishpond. It collapsed under her weight and she crashed sideways into the hole cracking her head on the corner of a large concrete block that was holding down the tarpaulin.

In the silence that followed Cynthia's eyes strained into the darkness. Something had happened. She forced herself upright, aware of the groans coming from the bottom of a hole she had miraculously stumbled by. Skirting around it she hobbled back to the dark house. Tumbling into the kitchen her shaking body fell against the slammed door. Her bloodied hands fumbled with the key and bolts.

The only light came from the flickering T.V. in the parlour doorway. "Oh God, Stanley." She stumbled to his room. She flicked on the light. He was lying on the bed in his red silk top and white underpants with black tape binding his wrists and stubs.

His face was a ghastly blue.

The icy water lying in the bottom of the hole stopped the bleeding on Lucy's gashed forehead and seemed to revive her. With numb fingers she tried to feel the deep cut as she struggled to crawl out of the slippery hole, lined with black plastic. Her bare feet kept sliding on it's freezing smooth surface. Reeling like a festive reveller she staggered back to the house. The door was locked, so was the entry gate. She loosened the frozen bolt with a half brick and stumbled down the black entry, hanging on to the narrow walls for support, trying to work out a new plan.

The crazy old woman who lived next door had always been jealous of her. She had wanted Stanley for herself and when he fell in love with another woman and married her, it tipped her over the edge. Cynthia wasn't the full ticket, ask anybody. Cynthia had planned to kill them both tonight. The evil bitch. She even had a key made for the back door. It was only by a stroke of luck she managed to escape. Her husband was already dead. The police must arrest this lunatic before she kills again.

Emerging from the entry into the street Lucy shouted to a small group of people on the other side of the road.

"Help, help me. Please help me."

The faces tuned as one towards the pleading, pathetic voice. They saw a bedraggled young woman in a torn nightdress limping towards them with bloody bare feet, her face and blond hair covered in blood. Anguished cries from a victim of abuse.

The driver of the car only started braking after the woman had smashed into his windscreen. Someone in the small group of people screamed at the broken body lying in the middle of the road.

CHAPTER
TWENTY SEVEN

In the bright sunshine on a Valentine's Day morning the white frost still glittered on the shaded parts of the lawn at 97 Albert Street. Inside, sitting at the red Formica table, Edith and Cynthia sipped their umpteenth cup of tea with half a packet of digestives laid out, begging to be dunked.

"Yes there is to be a documentary about him. That's in May. Then there's the book and now there's mention of a film." It was all too much for Edith.

"One cannot believe it my dear but *his* was a remarkable story. It should be told. It will make him famous."

"Stanley never liked the celebrity culture. A bunch of 'screaming yeahboys' he called them. It was always the simple life for him. Anyway, it's all too late now."

"What do you mean dear?"

"Well, at his age and the way that he is. I don't think he'll enjoy all the attention."

"Oh, I have noticed quite an improvement in him over the last week."

"It's not the physical side of recovery I'm worried about. He just doesn't seem interested in anything anymore. Just sits around, hardly talking. He's very lethargic, keeps forgetting things. I'm really quite worried about him at the moment."

"It's to be expected dear. These things must run their course."

"Yes I suppose I'm just being silly but I say a prayer for him every night."

Encased in a thick blanket, Stanley gulped in the dazzling sunshine while he listened to a robin's song as it flitted from tree to tree. The regular visitor to the garden always seemed curious in the sad statue with smoke coming out his mouth.

Stanley thought the extension looked smaller now it was finished. Empty, pink plastered rooms. Joyless, soulless. They had been built for him to share with his beautiful bride. That could never be now. She was dead. Her broken body lying in frozen earth, a short bus ride away. His brown eyes moistened with pain.

He wished he was dead too. Wished she had killed him on that Christmas Eve. At least then he would be free of this heartache. He felt like Humpty Dumpty. No-one could put his shattered heart back together again. No surgeon, living or unborn could sew together the broken, jagged edges to how they once were. No magic pill. No words of comfort existed that would cure him. Even if his heart was taken out and replaced he would still feel the pain of it's dying gasp. The ghost of his heart would live on inside him and so would Lucy's.

"Cooee, Stanley." The gaunt heroine with the Vulcan bomber hairstyle waved from the back door. There was no denying her over enthusiastic mouth to mouth resuscitating kiss had probably saved his life. It was what she wanted in return that worried him. He gave her the 'thumb's up' and edged further down the garden.

Still sleeping in a room where two people had tried to kill him should have worried him but it didn't. No-one would describe it as normal but he was past caring. He could never bring himself to sleep in the new 'honeymoon suite.' So he would stay in the front parlour room. Perhaps until he was carried out in the old proverbial wooden box.

Edith's voice carried down the garden. "Mr Soap is here to see you love."

Stanley waved him down.

George Soap's smile leapt ahead of his short fat steps and extended the 'mother of all' handshakes. "Great to see you again Stanley. I never thought being your agent would keep me so busy. Now, just to bring you up to date. The documentary is definitely going ahead in May. The first draft of your life story is back from the publisher's. They love it. Now, wait for it, the film rights have been sold. Doesn't get any better than that. We're talking millions Stanley."

He managed a weak smile. "That's fantastic George but I've already got millions."

"Famous then. The indestructible Stanley Kandlecake. The man they could not kill. Back from the dead, Three times. What a story."

"I don't want to sound ungrateful George but fame is for... Other people. You know the sort. You must deal with them everyday."

The short man with the tall smile, buried in a fur trimmed brown suede coat and matching hat raised both arms. "Immortal then. That's what you become once you're name's on that silver screen. Immortality. Would you settle for that?"

His smile was stronger this time. "Yes George, I would settle for that."

"Then just sign these papers for me Stanley and I will do

that not too small thing for you." He produced what looked like a rolled gold pen with his sheath of papers. Stanley scrawled his way through the endless sheets and reluctantly handed the 'hot' pen back to it's owner.

"I've always wanted a pen like that." He had the look of a little boy.

"Then keep it Stanley. Use it to for your first book signing."

It had been a long time since anyone had shown him any kindness. Given him a gift, apart from his mum. He held the beautiful gold missile in his hand and felt tears running down his face.

His agent looked on, lost for words, for once. "It's not real gold Stanley."

He chuckled. It doesn't matter George. It's a lovely gesture. It's been a strange old year, one way and another."

"I don't know how you're still alive."

Unable to talk, his mad sorting laugh was another release and more tears rolled down his face, his wet brown eyes pleading with George to blow his tormented brains out with a silver bullet. The small man with the big grin and big nose leaned over and hugged him. "It's all right Stanley, It's all over now."

They said goodbye with an affectionate handshake and another hug and he watched his agent's expensive brogue shoes crunch on the shaded, frosty grass with tentative steps. George turned at the walled gate. "Immortality Stanley, just like Achilles."

He waved back. Who? A heel? Ah, the Greek bloke. He wished he could be more like George or even be him. Let's do a swap. Give me your personality, The charm, the self assured, successful man and your legs and I will give you all my millions. He knew it wasn't a fair swap, burdening someone with this tortured heart.

All lumped together, the amputation of his legs, his cracked skull, the migraines, all this suffering and misery paled next to the aching emptiness gnawing at his insides. It had been explained to him, many times that Lucy had tried to kill him but why should that stop him still loving her? He felt foolish now, breaking down in front of George like that, who he hardly knew. God knows what he must have thought. Is that what he was having, a nervous breakdown? His terrible mood swings would support that.

The North wind blew sparks off the tip of his fat 'roll up' He sucked a lump of nicotine up into what was left of his brain and blew thin slivers of smoke at the small white clouds racing across the powder blue sky, carried by the high Arctic winds.

The thought of immortality perked him up, for a short while. A lost love is a strange thing. Some people die of a broken heart. He was told that years ago. It sounded plausible then. He believed it now.

The sun disappeared. Black clouds replaced the white clouds. The sky was suddenly grey. He pulled the blanket up tighter under his armpits. He loved being out in this wild weather. Loading bricks with his forklift now seemed a million years ago. Another life, another world. He wanted his old life back, his old world. Those lost days of petty, boring problems. Sanity and normality. How he wished for those days again, but they were gone forever, as if they never existed. Blown away like the high Arctic clouds. Fresh cold tears, chilled by the North wind hung on his eyelashes and rolled onto his lined face.

All those millions in the bank were useless to him now.

Happiness was not for sale. Nor was that feeling he used to get every morning waking up and seeing his new wife lying next to him. That surge of intense love for life and everything which kick started every day and lasted until he fell asleep again.

All those millions. He would have a purge. Give it all away. Most of it anyway. It might help someone out. The thought had a cleansing effect on him. Is this why he had been saved? To save other people through charitable acts with this unburdening of his millions. All very noble but he was aware of the power of money. Perhaps this would bring him a kind of peace. God knows he needed something. He used up his last precious matches relighting his 'roll up' in the gusty wind. The sky turned darker.

Despite the most horrible act someone can do against your person it won't stop you having strong emotional feelings of longing to be with them. How could that be? It didn't make any sense. It defied all logic. Love is a more complex emotion than hate. Hate is a one trick pony that feeds on fear. It destroys everything it touches and then devours the host it's living on. A cannibalistic parasite. It is an identifiable cancer, curable in some cases. Love is more deadly because it's identity is invisible, illogical and it has no cure.

His brain was starting to hurt. He dragged another mouthful of sweet tobacco down into his stumps. Love was like...*Alice in Wonderland*. Totally bonkers.

He felt more tired than usual today and his headache was worse than yesterday's. An exhausted sadness overwhelmed him. He closed his eyes over Lucy's face. He would rest for a while until the dizziness passed.

Seconds later his head slumped forward as flecks of snow formed on his blanket and hat. Within minutes the dark hunched figure trapped in his wheelchair and trapped in his mind was engulfed in a storm of snowflakes.

"Why not take a holiday Edith dear. It would invigorate both of you. Heaven knows you deserve it." Cynthia nibbled on a digestive like a constipated rabbit.

"I think I'll wait a while longer, he still seems so weak. We'll hang on for the warmer weather. We do get some nice days in Springtime."

"Yes I forgot he has no love for foreign climates."

"Never had a passport. He's got this thing about the French, especially. In the next breath he says he wouldn't mind visiting Agincourt or Crecy."

"Yes dear, he is a deep one, is our Stanley. Where is he, in the front parlour?"

"No, I don't think so. I didn't see him come in, did you?" They both looked out at the snowstorm. Fear gripped Edith's stomach. Her hands covered her mouth. "He must be still out there." They jumped up together and rushed outside.

At the bottom of the garden they could make out the snow covered outline of a figure slumped forward in his wheelchair. "Stanley, what are you doing out in this lot?" Edith's panicking shout received no reply.

Their footsteps slowed as they approached the white mound. "Stanley, can you hear me?" Edith lifted his lifeless head with the palms of her hands and wiped away the snow from his closed eyes and mouth. "Stanley, what's wrong?" She was crying now. "He's not moving, what's wrong?" The snowstorm threatened to overwhelm them. "Let's get him inside Edith."

"Stanley, Stanley." Edith was almost hysterical.

The snow on his eyelashes fluttered. His dark brown eyes slowly opened. They looked large in his white face.

190

"Oh God, I thought we had really lost you this time."

"It's all right mum." He whispered. The indestructible Stanley Kandlecake gave her his widest smile.

THE END